Suppression & Suspicion

T0043351

The chronicles of Hugh de Singleton, surgeon

MEL STARR

The fifteenth chronicle of Hugh de Singleton, surgeon

Suppression & Suspicion

LION FICTION

Text copyright © 2022 Mel Starr
This edition copyright © 2022 Lion Hudson IP Limited

The right of Mel Starr to be identified as the author of this work has
been asserted by him in accordance with the Copyright, Designs and
Patents Act 1988.

All rights reserved. No part of this publication may be reproduced or
transmitted in any form or by any means, electronic or mechanical,
including photocopy, recording, or any information storage and
retrieval system, without permission in writing from the publisher.

Published by
Lion Fiction
www.lionhudson.com
Part of the SPCK Group
SPCK, 36 Causton Street, London, SW1P 4ST

ISBN 978 1 78264 354 8
e-ISBN 978 1 78264 355 5

First edition 2022

Acknowledgments
Scripture quotations taken from the Authorized Version of the Bible
(The King James Bible), the rights in which are vested in the Crown,
and reproduced by permission of the Crown's Patentee, Cambridge
University Press.

A catalogue record for this book is available from the British Library

Printed and bound in United Kingdom, Clays Ltd, Bungay, Suffolk.

For Professor Dan Jensen

"The ideal condition would be, I admit, that men should be right by instinct; but since we are all likely to go astray, the reasonable thing is to learn from those who can teach."

Sophocles (c. 496–406 BC), *Antigone*

Acknowledgments

In 2007, when he learned that I had written an as yet unpublished medieval mystery, Dr. Dan Runyon, Professor of English at Spring Arbor University, invited me to speak to his fiction-writing class about the trials of a rookie writer seeking a publisher. He sent sample chapters of Hugh de Singleton's first chronicle to his friend Tony Collins at Lion Hudson. Thanks, Dan.

Tony has since retired, but many thanks to him and all those at Lion Hudson who saw Hugh de Singleton's potential.

Dr. John Blair, of Queen's College, Oxford, has written several papers about Bampton history. These have been valuable in creating an accurate time and place for Hugh.

In the summer of 1990 Susan and I found a delightful B&B in Mavesyn Ridware, a medieval village north of Lichfield. Proprietors Tony and Lis Page became friends, and when they moved to Bampton invited us to visit them there. Tony and Lis introduced me to Bampton and became a great source of information about the village. Tony died in March 2015, only a few months after being diagnosed with cancer. He is greatly missed.

Glossary

Aloes of lamb: lamb sliced thinly and rolled in a mixture of egg yolk, suet, onion, and various spices, then baked.

Ambler: an easy riding horse, because it moved both right legs together, then both left legs.

Angelus: a devotional celebrated three times each day, at dawn, noon, and dusk, announced by the ringing of the church bell.

Arbolettys: a cheese and herb egg custard.

Bail: an arched handle of a pail or kettle.

Bailiff: a lord's chief manorial representative. He oversaw all operations, collected rents and fines, and enforced labor service. Not a popular fellow.

Bailiwick: a bailiff's jurisdiction.

Beadle: a manor official in charge of fences, hedges, enclosures, and curfew. He served under the reeve. Also called a hayward.

Blancmange: literally "white food". A mixture of rice, almonds, lard, salt, and perhaps sugar and ginger. Worked to softness, then ground to a smooth paste.

Braes: medieval underpants.

Buck: a male fallow deer, not so large or prized as the stag/hart, a male red deer.

Burgher: a town merchant or tradesman.

Buttery: a room for beverages stored in "butts", or barrels.

Canabeans: soak beans in cold water, strip off hulls, then simmer for ninety minutes with bacon.

Capon farced: a castrated male chicken stuffed with hard-boiled egg yolks, currants, chopped pork, breadcrumbs, and spices.

Chauces: tight-fitting trousers, often of different colors for each leg.

Chicken in bruit: chicken cubed, then simmered in a stock of wine, breadcrumbs, ginger, pepper, and saffron.

Compost: a vegetable and fruit casserole, often including cabbage, parsnips, turnips, pears, and currants, flavored with honey, spices, and wine.

Coppice (v.): to cut a tree back so that a thicket of small saplings would grow from the stump. These shoots were used for everything from arrows to rafters, depending on how much they were permitted to grow.

Cormarye: roast pork with spices, seasoning, garlic, and wine.

Cotehardie: the primary medieval outer garment. Women's were floor-length; men's ranged from mid-thigh to ankle.

Cotter: a poor villager, usually holding five acres or fewer. He often had to labor for wealthier villagers to make ends meet.

Couching: excising the clouded lens from the eye of a cataract sufferer.

Daub: a clay and plaster mix, reinforced with straw and/or horsehair. Applied over wattles to make a wall.

Demesne: land directly exploited by a lord, and worked by his villeins, as opposed to land rented to tenants.

Dexter: a war horse, larger than a runcie or palfrey. Sometimes called a destrier. Also, the right-hand direction.

Eels in bruit: eels cut into small pieces, served in a sauce of white wine, breadcrumbs, onions, and spices.

Farthing: one-fourth of a penny. The smallest silver coin.

Fast day: Wednesday, Friday, and Saturday. Not fasting in modern terms, when no food is consumed, but days when no meat, eggs, or animal products were consumed. Fish was on the menu for those who could afford it.

Fewterer: keeper of a lord's kennels and hounds.

Fraunt hemelle: an egg, minced pork, and breadcrumb pudding. Ingredients were mixed, boiled in a sack, then briefly grilled.

Froise and cryspes: a mixture of flour, egg whites, lard, milk, sugar, salt, and yeast. The batter was fried in the lard.

Galyntine sauce: a thick sauce, usually for pork, made of red wine vinegar, onions, bread crumbs, lard, and spices.

Gathering: eight leaves of parchment, made by folding the prepared hide three times.

Gentleman: a nobleman. The term had nothing to do with character or behavior.

Groat: a silver coin worth four pence.

Groom: a lower-rank servant to a lord, occasionally a teenaged youth. Ranked above a page but below a valet.

Haberdasher: a merchant who sold household items such as pins, buckles, hats, and purses.

Hallmote: the manor court. It had jurisdiction over legal matters concerning villagers, but it was usually royal courts that judged tenants charged with murder.

Heriot: an inheritance tax paid to the lord of the manor, usually the heir's best animal.

Houpeland: a long, tailored garment with high waist and collar and long, elaborate sleeves. Generally worn only by upper classes.

Hue and cry: alarm raised by the person who discovered a crime. All who heard were expected to go to the scene of the crime and, if possible, pursue the felon.

Infangenthef: the right of a lord of a manor to judge and execute a thief caught in the act.

King's Eyre: a royal circuit court, usually presided over by a traveling judge.

Kirtle: the basic medieval undershirt.

Lady: wife to a gentleman. As with her husband, the title had nothing to do with character or behavior.

Ladywell: a well dedicated to the Virgin Mary located a short distance north of Bampton Castle, the water of which was reputed to cure ills, especially of the eye.

Leach lombard: a dish of ground pork, eggs, raisins, currants, and dates, with spices added. The mixture was boiled in a sack until set, then sliced for serving.

Lychgate: a roofed gate in the churchyard wall under which the deceased rested during the initial part of a burial service.

Lymer: a scenting hound.

Madder: a plant, the roots of which were used to make a red dye.

Marshalsea: the stables and associated accoutrements.

Martinmas: November 11. The traditional date to slaughter animals for winter food.

Maslin: bread made with a mixture of grains, commonly wheat with barley or rye.

Mattock: a tool with a pick at one side of the implement and an adze on the other.

Michaelmas: September 29. The feast signaled the end of the harvest, when last rents and tithes were due.

Page: a young male servant – often a youth learning the arts of chivalry before becoming a squire.

Palfrey: a riding horse with a comfortable gait.

Pannage: a fee paid to a lord for permission to allow pigs to forage in an autumn forest.

Pantry: from the French word for bread, "pain". Originally a small room for bread storage, but by the fourteenth century other items were also stored there.

Parapet: the upper level of a castle wall.

Pax board: frequently painted with sacred scenes, this object was passed through the congregation during a service for all to kiss. Literally, "peace board".

Penny: the most common medieval coin; made of silver. Twelve pennies made a shilling and twenty shillings made a pound, although there were no shilling or pound coins.

Porre of peas: peas simmered until they burst, then in cold water the hulls are rubbed off. Returned to stock with chopped onions, salt, sugar, and saffron. Served hot.

Portpain: a linen cloth in which bread was carried from a castle bakehouse or pantry to the hall.

Pottage: anything cooked in one pot, from the meanest gruel to a savory stew.

Ravioles: pastries filled with cheese, beaten eggs, occasionally minced pork or poultry, and spices, then boiled.

Reeve: an important manor official, although he did not outrank the bailiff. Elected by tenants from among themselves – often the best husbandman – he was responsible for fields, buildings, and labor service.

Runcie: a small common horse of a lower grade than a palfrey.

St. Andrew's Chapel: an ancient chapel a few hundred yards east of Bampton, dating to before the Norman Conquest.

St. Beornwald's Church: today the Church of St. Mary the Virgin, in the fourteenth century it was dedicated to an obscure Saxon saint enshrined in the church.

Sinister: the left-hand direction.

Skin window: animal skin treated with oil so as to be translucent.

Solar: a small private room, more easily heated than the great hall, where lords often preferred to spend time, especially in winter. Usually on an upper floor.

Sops in fennel: bread toasted, then covered with a syrup of fennel, saffron, onions, salt, olive oil, sugar, and cinnamon.

Stag: a male red deer, also called a hart.

Statute of Laborers: following the first attack of plague in 1348–49, laborers realized that because so many workers had died, their labor was in short supply, so they demanded higher wages. In 1351 parliament set wages at the 1347 level. Like most attempts to legislate against the law of supply and demand, the statute was generally a failure. A later statute also attempted to regulate rents and tenancy.

Stockfish: inexpensive fish, usually dried cod or haddock, consumed on fast days.

Stone: fourteen pounds.

Surplice: a loose white outer vestment, usually of knee length, with large open sleeves.

Tenant: a free peasant who rented land from his lord. He could pay his rent in labor or, more likely by the fourteenth century, in cash.

Dramatis personae

Hugh de Singleton	Surgeon, bailiff to Lord Gilbert, and sleuth
Lady Katherine (Kate)	Hugh de Singleton's wife
Bessie and John Singleton	Their children
Adela Parkin	Hugh and Kate's servant
Stephen Parkin	Adela's father, tenant of Lord Gilbert
Emmaline Parkin	Adela's mother
Lord Gilbert	Third Baron Talbot
Lady Petronilla Talbot	Lord Gilbert's late wife
Richard Talbot	Their son
Charles de Burgh	Lord Gilbert's nephew
Sir Jaket Bec	Household knight to Lord Talbot
Thomas	Squire to Sir Jaket
Sir William Daubney	Lord Gilbert's marshal
John Chamberlain	Lord Gilbert's chamberlain
Arthur Wagge	Groom to Lord Gilbert (deceased)
Cicely Wagge	His wife, servant to Lord Gilbert
Janyn Wagge	Cicely and Arthur's son, servant to Lord Gilbert
Uctred	Ancient groom to Lord Gilbert
Rolf and Beatrice Toty	Tenants of Lord Gilbert
Peg and Godwin Tyrrell	Tenants of Lord Gilbert
Thomas Neckham	A poor cotter, swineherd

Toft: land surrounding a house, often used for growing vegetables.

Trencher: a platter of wood or bread for serving food.

Valet: a high-ranking servant to a lord.

Verderer: in charge of a lord's forests.

Verjuice: the juice of crab apples, used sparingly to flavor sauces.

Vicar: a priest serving a parish but, unlike a rector, not entitled to its tithes.

Villein: a non-free peasant. He could not leave his land or service to his lord, or sell animals without permission. But if he could escape his manor for a year and a day he would be free.

Wattle: interlaced sticks used as a foundation and support for daub when building a wall.

Week work: the two or three days of work per week owed to a lord by a villein.

Woad: a plant whose leaves produced a blue dye.

Yardland: thirty or so acres. Also called a virgate, and in northern England an oxgang.

Edmund Harkins	Tenant farmer
Leuca Harkins	Edmund's wife
Ewen Lusk	Leuca's brother
Walter atte Brook	Member of Edmund Hawkins' plough team
Osbert atte Brook	Member of Edmund Hawkins' plough team
Father Thomas	Priest, St. Beornwald's Church
Christopher	Father Thomas's clerk
Father Ralph	Priest, St. Beornwald's Church
Father Harold Brantyngham	Priest, St. Beornwald's Church, and the Bishop of Exeter's nephew
Randall Creten	Father Harold's clerk
John Kellet	Priest, St. Andrew's Chapel
John Prudhomme	Bampton's reeve
Will Shillside	Bampton's haberdasher
Robert Baker	Bampton's baker
Maud Baker	Robert's wife
Philip Carpenter	Bampton's carpenter
John Whitestaff	Bampton's beadle
Bampton's holy man	
Sir Roger Wren	From Bath, visiting Lord Gilbert
Lady Wren	Sir Roger's wife
Rohilda Wren	Their daughter
Sir Reginald Stury	Lord of Curbridge

N

1. Galen House
2. The Church of St. Beornwald
3. blacksmith's forge
4. to St. Andrew's Chapel
5. the Ladywell

6. Bampton Castle
7. Cowley's Corner
8. the mill
9. marketplace
10. The holy man's hut

• 5.

6.

■ 10.

?.

Mill

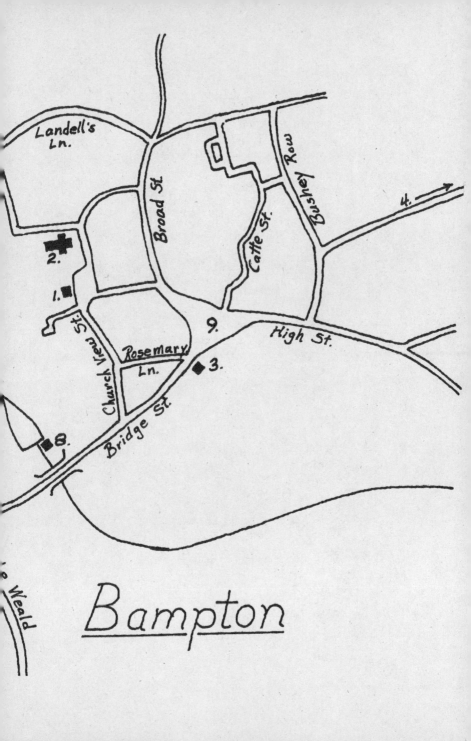

Chapter 1

'Twas the fourth day of October, the Feast of St. Francis of Assisi, in the year of our Lord one thousand, three hundred and seventy-six. I walked the muddy bank of Shill Brook, to the south of Bampton, where I knew I would find a grove of willows and likely some monk's hood. Both of these may be used to relieve pain, though I will not use monk's hood but as a rub. The plant's root, ground fine and mixed with oil, will alleviate an aching joint. And blended into a cup of ale the powdered root is a strong sedative. But too much becomes a deadly poison. The bark of the willow, dried and powdered and added to a cup of ale, is a safer physic. It is not so effective as hemp seeds, but easier to come by, and no man will die from quaffing a cup of ale imbued with fragments of willow bark. He may if his physician offers a dose of monk's hood. I will not do so, no matter what hurt my patient may be suffering.

I am Hugh de Singleton, surgeon, and bailiff to Lord Gilbert, Third Baron Talbot, at his manor of Bampton – Sir Hugh, since Prince Edward of Woodstock granted me a knighthood some years past for service I rendered. He had sent for me to attend him at Kennington Palace because whilst at the siege of Limoges I had offered him some herbs which relieved his infirmity. Whilst I attended the prince at Kennington, a knight in his service was slain and I discovered the murderer. For these services I was made Sir Hugh, and my wife is Lady Katherine, although to me she will always be Kate.

I had with me as I prowled the bank of Shill Brook two sacks; one for willow bark, the other for the root of monk's hood. So hazardous is monk's hood I will not allow it to mingle in the same sack with willow bark. Mayhap this is an excess of caution, but few men have suffered from too much discretion. As the willow bark is much the easier to collect, I filled that sack first, then sought the monk's hood. I drew from the soil three plants, shook the dirt from the roots, placed them in the smaller bag, and turned for home.

I met Will Shillside, Bampton's haberdasher, as I walked from Bridge Street to Church View Street. He also had a sack slung over his shoulder. He had departed Bampton early Friday morning to replenish his stock of pins and buckles and ribbons and such. He was no doubt pleased to be home. Roads are unsafe. King Edward is in his dotage and seems to care for little but his mistress, Alice Perrers. And his heir, Edward of Woodstock, died in June. My physics could alleviate, but they could not cure. Our next king will be Prince Edward's son, Richard of Bordeaux. The lad is but nine years old. When his grandfather dies, who, I wonder, will be regent? His mother Joan, or his wily uncle, John of Gaunt?

"What news?" I hailed when Will came near.

"Prince Edward was buried five days past in Canterbury Cathedral," he replied, "although the funeral will not be held 'til Monday."

My employer, Lord Gilbert Talbot, had set off for Canterbury ten days past, accompanied by several of his household knights and valets. Perhaps he would return in a week's time, if no other business in London or Oxford delayed him.

"Does plague yet afflict Oxford?" I asked.

"Not so much," Will replied.

The pestilence had returned a year past. Not so many perished as when the disease first struck, but Bampton lost seven souls in the return, including Arthur Wagge, a groom to Lord Gilbert, who had often assisted me when I required his strength and wit to subdue malefactors. Father Simon, one of the three priests who served the collegiate Church of St. Beornwald, also perished. Father Thomas and Father Ralph told me a few days past that they expected Father Simon's replacement to arrive soon. The Bishop of Exeter had been lax in appointing a man, as there were yet two priests to serve the parish.

I bade Will good day and set off for Galen House and my dinner. 'Twas a fast day, so there was no flesh in the pot or upon a spit. Kate and Adela had prepared sops in fennel.

We had just finished the meal when I heard a scream. The sound was faint, as the day was cool and the doors and windows of Galen House were closed against a chill breeze.

I looked to Kate and we shared an unspoken understanding. Edmund Harkins was again beating his wife. Kate has remonstrated with me that I do something to put a stop to this regular occurrence, but what can a bailiff do? The law permits a husband "lawful and reasonable correction" of his wife. I could bring Edmund before hallmote, but to what purpose? Men of Bampton would surely impose no penalty, as some of them too had likely given their wife a swat when she displeased them. Of course, if they did so, they might dine upon cold pottage for a week. The weaker sex is not without some strength.

When we heard Leuca screech, our conversation ceased, but when there was no following yelp we resumed speech. The convivial banter, however, was now dampened. Kate's lips were pursed. I am a man of authority in Bampton. She desired that I use that power to restrain Edmund.

I had spoken to the man in the past about his mistreatment of his wife. His response was to glare at me, spit upon the ground, and turn away. At first the beatings occurred in the evenings, when he had consumed too much ale, but of late we were likely to hear Leuca's screams at any time. As today.

The chill autumn air had penetrated Galen House and settled over our dinner table. Bessie sensed this and glanced from the corner of her eye to me, then to her mother. John was oblivious, licking his lips and looking to the empty trencher where a few moments earlier our dinner had been.

"I will walk past Rosemary Lane," I said. "Mayhap if I see Edmund and scowl he will know that his malign behavior has attracted attention."

"He has attracted attention in such manner for years," Kate scoffed. "And many have scowled at him. To what purpose?"

'Twas a valid question, for which I had no ready reply. If a man chooses to beat his wife neither his lord nor his lord's bailiff has authority to intervene, unless some permanent injury should result. I had noticed that the oldest child, a lad of about eight years, was beginning to exhibit a disagreeable disposition. Like father, like son. If there were ways I could, with what powers I do possess, make Edmund's life unpleasant I would apply them. But whatever methods I might undertake would do harm to the entire family, to Leuca and the three children.

I observed that Kate consumed but a small portion of

the sops in fennel. Was she so angry that she had lost her appetite? Nay. We heard Leuca's howl when dinner was near done, not before.

I departed Galen House with no destination in mind but to pass Rosemary Lane and flee Kate's ire. Her wrath would not last long. I know my Kate. She is quick to complain of injustice, but also quick to forgive.

I walked from Church View Street to Rosemary Lane and slowed my pace. I hoped to see Edmund so that I could exchange insults with the scoundrel but instead I saw Leuca. She sat before her house on a crude bench and shelled peas from a late planting. The woman looked up to see who passed and I saw a streak of blood above her left eyebrow. I approached her.

When I came near I saw that the flesh above Leuca's eyebrow was split the length of the brow. The wound no longer dripped blood into her eye, but it had, for I saw a red stain upon the brown cotehardie she wore. The split was red, and no scab had formed. The cut was recent. Here was the cause of the cry which had interrupted the conclusion of my dinner.

"How did your injury happen?" I asked.

"Stumbled on t' threshold," Leuca replied.

Edmund heard my question and appeared in the open doorway. "Clumsy," he said. "Fell against yon bench." He nodded toward the dim interior of the house. As Edmund spoke I saw him rub the knuckles of his right hand.

"Such a wound should be stitched," I said. "If left as is 'twill leave an ugly scar."

"Bah," Edmund snorted. "You be lookin' for coins."

"Leuca cannot see the gash, but if she could she would want it dealt with. 'Tis a husband's duty to care for his wife. Two pence to close the cut."

I would have asked for more, six pence at least, but I knew Edmund would not agree to his wife's treatment if I demanded my usual fee. And Leuca had enough to deal with, living with Edmund. She did not need an unsightly scar disfiguring her face.

"Come with me to Galen House," I said to the woman.

"Wait," Edmund said. "I ain't said I'd pay."

"What rent do you pay Lord Gilbert for your fields? A yardland, is it?"

"Eight shillin's," he muttered.

"A small enough fee for good land. Mayhap I should discuss your rent with Lord Gilbert when he returns."

"Tuppence, you say, to deal with Leuca's cut?"

"Aye. And the work must be done now, before a scar begins to form."

"Do what you must," he shrugged, and turned away.

Leuca set her peas aside and followed me to Galen House.

I sent Adela to the castle with instructions to seek John Chamberlain and return with a small flagon of wine. I told the maid to explain why I needed it. The chamberlain would not begrudge the donation from Lord Gilbert's butts. I intended to bathe the wound with wine before and after I stitched it closed. A wound cleansed with wine will heal better than one not so treated, though no man knows why.

I sat Leuca upon a bench whilst I went to my chest and returned with a fine needle and a length of silken thread. My chest is in a separate room, and while I was there I heard Kate speaking to Leuca, but so softly I could not understand the conversation. I learned later of the exchange.

Adela returned, breathless, with the wine and I proceeded to wash the cut and close it. Leuca bore the sting of the wine and needle well, so I used more stitches than might have been necessary. Many small sutures leave less of a scar than a few large stitches. The woman had borne Edmund's blows and given birth to three children, so I suppose she was accustomed to pain, and the prick of my needle was bearable.

I bathed the closed wound again with wine, bade the woman good day, and sent her home. I would collect the two pence from Edmund at some later time. Perhaps.

"What did Leuca tell you of her injury?" Kate asked when the woman was away.

"Said she stumbled over the threshold and fell against a bench."

"Did you believe her?"

"A fall could cause such a wound."

"Was Edmund present to hear her explanation?"

"Aye, he was. Hmm. I see your drift. If his fist had opened the wound she would hesitate to tell the bailiff. If she spoke the truth she might receive another blow for her honesty."

"Just so. While you were collecting needle and thread Leuca told me 'twas Edmund's blow that opened her cut. Something must be done. She said his fits of rage grow more frequent. One day I fear he will slay her."

"Then he will hang."

"Little good that will do Leuca. Can you do nothing to end his savagery?"

"I threatened to increase his rent if he would not permit me to close Leuca's wound. Mayhap such a warning might reduce his violence, but if he strikes her when drunk he will not have wits enough to consider the consequences."

"So you will do nothing?" Kate said.

"I did not say so. When Lord Gilbert returns from Canterbury I will seek him and ask his permission to double Edmund's rent if he raises his hand to Leuca again. I believe he will agree to the threat. John Chamberlain told me some months past that Lord Gilbert is heavily in debt. Maintaining three castles is expensive. Rents, since so many tenants have perished, do not meet expenses. And I must admit my employer is something of a spendthrift."

"Your words will not be repeated," Kate smiled. "Lord Gilbert would not want his finances known to folk of his manor."

My supper that evening was simple. I have not read in my Bible that the Lord Christ requires men to abstain from flesh and eggs and cheese three days each week. We are told that upon occasion we should fast and pray, but no schedule is given.

Kate and Adela had prepared a porre of peas, a meal which, even if not flavored with a bit of pork, is a reasonable substitute for something more nourishing.

Edmund, Leuca, and their children passed Galen House on their way to St. Beornwald's Church Sunday morning. I was just then leaving my home with Kate and Bessie and John. I studied Leuca's wound as she passed, seeking any sign of redness or puss. Some physicians claim that thick white puss issuing from a wound is good – laudable pus, 'tis called – and a thin watery pus is dangerous. But I hold, along with Henri de Mondeville, that no pus at all seeping from a wound is best. And wounds should not be painted with salve, as they heal best when open to the air. I have had success following his opinion.

Edmund saw me studying his wife and scowled. Here was nothing unusual. Edmund scowls at most folk, most of the time.

"Leuca was once beautiful," Kate whispered as the family passed by.

"Aye," I replied, "but what time has not ravaged, Edmund has."

I had business Sunday evening with John Prudhomme, Bampton's reeve, and when 'twas done I returned to Galen House by way of Rosemary Lane. I decided to visit Leuca for a closer inspection of the wound. I'd had but a passing glance in the morning.

The woman was ladling pease pottage from a pot bubbling upon the hearthstone. Edmund said nothing about the tuppence owed, but ignored me, bent over his bowl, belched, and then drank from a cup of ale. Leuca immediately refilled the cup from a stained leather ewer. After a brief inspection of her wound I left the family to their supper. There was some redness about Leuca's cut, but no pus, laudable or otherwise.

Lord Gilbert's tenants and villeins were busy Monday morning at the last plowing of autumn. I, with John Prudhomme, walked the fields making sure that the plow teams working Lord Gilbert's demesne lands set furrows deep enough to expose the roots of weeds.

I returned to Galen House for my dinner. Kate and Adela had prepared fraunt hemelle. I ate my fill but was concerned that Kate took only a small portion. The dish was one of her favorites.

I rose from the table, stretched, finished what ale remained in my cup, then heard a rapping upon Galen House door. I opened it to find Leuca Harkins.

My first thought was that the cut above her eye had festered, or was causing her pain. A glance at the sutures told me all was well. Had Edmund struck her again, and she now sought succor from his blows? I saw no evidence of that. Her eye below the wound was purpled and would remain so for a few days, but her face bore no sign of new injury, nor did she carry herself stiffly, as if her ribs gave her grief.

"I give you good day, Leuca. How may I serve you?"

"'Tis Edmund. 'E didn't return from plowin' for 'is dinner, so I sought Walter and Osbert."

"They are a plow team with Edmund?"

"Aye. Said 'e'd not been at work this morn."

"And he's not sought his dinner? When did you last see him? This morning, when he departed for plowing?"

"Nay. Odd thing. 'E was away when I awoke."

"You'd best come in and sit," I said, "and tell me all."

The woman entered and I pointed to a bench in the hall. Leuca sat at one end, and I the other. Kate peered through the doorway.

"Edmund left your bed before dawn without awakening you? Did he do this often?" I asked.

"Nay. Right surprised, I was. Most mornin's 'e's slug-a-bed. 'Specially if he's 'ad much ale night before."

"Had he consumed much ale Sunday evening?"

"Aye. So much 'e fell to bed without findin' some fault w' me an' layin' a hand to me or a kick to me backside."

"He departed so silently that neither you nor your children were awakened?"

"'E did. The bar was moved from the door. I thought 'im an' Osbert an' Walter planned to start plowin' at first light, days bein' shorter now an' not so much time to get a man's labor done."

"Has Edmund ever missed his dinner before?"

"Nay. Never off 'is feed, is Edmund."

Chapter 2

*L*euca had rapped upon Galen House door two or three times each day since Tuesday seeking news, of which I had none. So when I heard a pounding upon my door Friday morning I assumed 'twas her again. Not so.

Bampton's holy man stood before me. No man knows his name, for he will not speak. Whilst upon pilgrimage in Spain some years past he lost his way and strayed into Granada, where he fell afoul of Mussulmen. They enslaved him, and when he would not embrace Mohammed as a prophet of God, they tore out his tongue for his heresy.

After some months he managed to escape his captors and return to England, where he sought to enter some monastery as a lay brother. But due to his mutilation none would have him. It took months of asking him questions, which could be answered with only a nod or shake of the head, before I learned the fellow's history.

He first appeared in Bampton nearly two years past. He sat where Church View Street joins Bridge Street and with a soiled hand upon their heads made the sign of a blessing upon children who passed by. Parents were at first suspicious of the man garbed in a ragged cotehardie, shoeless, and with unkempt, matted hair and beard. But after a few days they began to provide gifts to repay his kindness: an egg or two, maslin loaves, a small sack of oats or beans.

"I'll seek Walter and Osbert this afternoon. Mayhap Edmund will appear in the meantime. If he does not return for his supper let me know."

My first thought as Leuca departed Galen House was that Edmund had decided to abandon family and responsibilities. This would not have surprised me. He was a tenant, not a villein, so no law held him to Bampton. And since plague has come and come again, laborers are in short supply. The Statute of Laborers attempted to fix wages to their customary level of 1348, before the pestilence felled so many. But like all such attempts to control men's finances, the statute has largely been a failure. Edmund could flee to Banbury or Swindon, or even London, and hire himself to some burgher. No questions would be asked.

Walter and Osbert had not seen Edmund since Sunday, and were disgusted with the man for shirking his share of their labor.

As the sun dropped below the browning leaves of Lord Gilbert's forest to the west, Leuca reappeared at Galen House. Edmund had not returned for his supper. The woman was in much distress. She evidently believed a bad husband better than none at all. There are, I am sure, wives who disagree.

Three days later Edmund had yet not returned, and Leuca was frantic. Town gossips presumed that he had absconded, and rumors of Leuca's unfitness as a wife provided his motive. The disappearance mystified me. I did not call for the hue and cry, as there was no evidence that a felony was involved in his disappearance.

Until Friday.

The holy man had found a shelter near Cowley's Corner, where in the forest he discovered a decayed swineherd's hut, which he repaired. It was his practice to defy curfew and prowl Bampton's streets in the night. This vexed me when I first discovered it, but I eventually told Bampton's beadle to allow the fellow to go unchallenged in the night. He could be relied upon to report to me any surreptitious activity he discovered in the night and I decided that his nocturnal perambulations might prove useful – if I could interpret the nodding and shaking of his head with which he tried to impart knowledge.

So they did. The holy man saw when the cook who had slain several of the clerks to the vicars of St. Beornwald's Church returned one night to collect his family. The felonious cook had some days past fled Bampton when he suspected I had discovered his villainy.

The holy man assisted me in capturing the rogue, and for this service Lord Gilbert rewarded the fellow by having the dilapidated hut demolished and replaced with a small house with walls of wattle and daub, a thatched roof, and a hearthstone where the man could boil his pottage out of the wind and rain.

I greeted the unkempt fellow and he motioned with a finger that I should follow him. He seemed agitated, as if there was some urgency to this request. There was.

We hastened past the castle to the path which led from the road to his tiny abode. Forty or so paces into the forest the holy man pointed to an opening in the trees and I followed him into the gap. Through the thinning autumn foliage I saw a man standing, a long rod in his hand. He heard our approach and turned his gaze toward us. When we drew near I saw that he stood over a small mound of earth and leaves. In the distance I heard the grunting and scrabbling of pannaging pigs. His staff told me the man was a swineherd, and when but five or six paces from him I saw 'twas Thomas Neckham, a poor cotter of the bishop's lands in the Weald. Some man, I thought, had hired Thomas to watch his pigs. But why should this concern me?

"Hello, Thomas. I give you good day," I greeted the swineherd. I was puzzled as to why the holy man had led me to this place, and why Thomas seemed to be expecting me. I soon learned the answer to both questions.

The pile of earth and leaves at Thomas's feet had been, I saw, removed from a shallow pit. At the bottom of this hole, which was less than the length of my forearm deep, I saw some strange mixture of brown and red and white tints.

I could not at first identify this colorful mass. When I did, I stepped back in horror. Here were the torn, bloody, dirt-crusted entrails of a man. I made the sign of the cross, then stepped closer for a better look, curiosity replacing my initial shock.

No face was visible, nor were legs and feet seen. The only flesh visible was of some man's body from chest to groin, and this much mutilated and eviscerated. Ribs and spine stood white against the dirt and offal. The remainder of the corpse was yet under the earth, which acted as a burial shroud.

"Me pigs found 'im," Thomas said, anticipating my question. "'Eard 'em rootin' about an' followed to see what they'd got to. Chased 'em away when I seen this."

"You've stood watch since," I asked, "to keep the pigs from this corpse?"

"Aye. But for a moment. I knew the holy man was close by, so ran to 'is 'ut an' told 'im to fetch you. Then I come back 'ere."

I knelt in the leaves and with my hand began to scoop soft earth and leaves from the dead man's face. I thought I could guess who rested here. I was right. I peered into the face of Edmund Harkins. But for the voracious pigs he might have remained in the forest 'til nothing but his bones awaited the Lord Christ's return.

Thoughts of what I must do tumbled through my mind. The corpse must be unearthed and returned to Leuca. A priest must be called and Edmund shriven. Lord Gilbert would soon return and must immediately be told of this murder, for felony this death surely was. And Will Shillside must collect his coroner's jury. Will was chosen coroner at hallmote some years past to replace his deceased father. Will is young for such a post, but wisdom is not always a fruit of age. More's the pity.

Thomas Neckham's round, simple face was pale with shock. I feared the fellow might swoon and fall upon Edmund's corpse.

"Remain here," I said to Thomas, "and keep the pigs far away. I'm off to collect Will Shillside, and thence to the castle to collect grooms to remove Edmund from this grave. Stay here also," I instructed the holy man, "and assist Thomas."

Whoso owned the swine which had gorged themselves upon Edmund's entrails might learn of their feasting. Would he then consume pork which had been fattened upon a man? I resolved to discover from Thomas whose pigs he cared for and instruct Kate and Adela not to purchase hams or bacon from the man.

I hurried to the castle and sought John Chamberlain. In Lord Gilbert's absence I would seek castle grooms only with his knowledge. I found him greeting visitors newly arrived. I was introduced to Sir Roger Wren, his lady wife, and their nubile daughter Rohilda.

My employer had lived alone, but for his nearly grown son, since the death by plague of his wife Petronilla. I could guess the reason for this visit. Sir Roger likely sought a good match for his daughter. Did he know of Lord Gilbert's debts? Who can say? Most of the barons of the realm live beyond their means, and since Edward I drove out the Jews, there are few ways for the nobility to raise cash upon a pledge. Evidently Sir Roger expected Lord Gilbert's imminent return. As did I.

I told John, who knew of Edmund Harkins' disappearance, of the discovery of his remains. "I need a few grooms to retrieve the corpse and take it to Leuca."

"Do what is necessary," he replied, then gave his attention to the castle guests.

I sought Uctred, a wizened old groom who had in the past assisted me and his friend Arthur in apprehending miscreants.

But the first man I saw crossing the castle yard was Sir Jaket Bec. He appeared to be on his way to the marshalsea, but changed his path when he saw me.

"I give you good day, Sir Hugh. What brings you to the castle this day?"

"Do you know of the missing tenant, Edmund Harkins?"

"Aye. Ran off leaving wife and family, the rascal. Though from what I've heard the woman may be well rid of him."

"She is indeed rid of him. His corpse is in a shallow grave no more than fifty paces from the holy man's hut. I seek Uctred and a few other grooms to fetch the dead man and take him to his wife."

"Uctred is in the marshalsea, mucking out. I'll let him know you need him. I and my squire will accompany him. Near to the holy man's hut, you say? I'll seek a pallet and we'll join you there shortly."

"Wait at the grave 'til I return. I must seek Father Thomas and the coroner. Will must convene his jury and view the corpse. The priest must meet us at Rosemary Lane and perform Extreme Unction for Edmund. If ever a man needed the sacrament 'twas Edmund."

I hurried from the castle, trotted up Bridge Street, thence to Church View Street, where I paused at Galen House to tell Kate of Edmund's fate. Then I hastened to Bushy Row, where I found Will Shillside and told him of his obligation. He promised to hurry to the grave. From Bushy Row I proceeded with haste to Father Thomas's vicarage.

"Dead in a shallow grave!" the priest exclaimed. "Few will mourn his passing, but all men are worthy of God's grace, whatever others may think of them."

"If they repent of their sins," I said.

"Aye. I'll fetch my clerk and go to Leuca."

"Wait there. Sir Jaket and I will bring Edmund to you."

"And then you must seek a murderer. Is this not so?"

"Aye, 'tis what my post requires."

"Some years past you were called to a similar duty. . . to find the felon who slew an evil man. All knew the malefactor might be a man respected in the town, and few were sorry the miscreant was dead. You will not find much cooperation in learning who has slain Edmund Harkins, I think."

"True. Nevertheless, I must do it. Lord Gilbert will likely return today or tomorrow. He must not find me shirking my duty merely because 'tis unpleasant."

"You will pardon me if I hope you fail," the priest said softly. "We are to show mercy, even to those who show none. But a priest is also a man, and may the Lord Christ forgive me for not attaining His perfection."

"Indeed. We all fail therein."

"Do I sin when I wish you no success in discovering who has slain Edmund?"

"Why ask me? I am a surgeon. You are the priest."

"Aye. Well, I will meet you at Leuca's house. Will you tell her of Edmund's death, or must I?"

"You will be there before we can exhume Edmund's corpse and take it to Rosemary Lane."

"So I will tell her of this sad business. I wonder, will she be sorrowful to be no longer abused?"

"You will have to ask her," I said. "I am off to retrieve the corpse. We will meet at Rosemary Lane."

When I arrived at Edmund's grave Sir Jaket, his squire, and Uctred had completely uncovered the corpse and laid it upon a canvas pallet supported by two poles, which two men could lift to carry away the body. This is what Uctred and the squire were about to do.

I told them to wait. Will Shillside and his jury would soon arrive and I wished to inspect the corpse, which I had not been able to do properly whilst it lay in the shallow grave. And I did not want to examine Edmund at his house, where Leuca might look on as I probed and poked, seeking a telltale wound or injury.

Edmund had been hastily interred. Whoso slew him did not trouble themselves to remove his clothes, although his shoes were gone. I examined cotehardie, kirtle, and braes for any sign of a penetrating wound, but found nothing. Of course, with the swine having done their work, such punctures and rips might well be obscured. The clothing was in great disarray.

I next felt Edmund's skull for any indication that he had received a blow. All seemed well. I found no lump, nor soft place where bone might be fractured. Nor was there a laceration hidden in Edmund's matted hair. He was dead, but the cause I could not determine. Had murder been done? Surely. Why else bury him in a place unlikely to be discovered? Had the rogue died of some affliction common to men, there would be no reason to conceal his demise.

He had left his bed early Monday morning, Leuca said. Why? Did he meet some man in the dark hour before dawn? If so, who? And for what purpose? And did such an encounter result in his death? A death with no cause I could discover.

I stood from examining the corpse, stretched, and rubbed my back. A few years past such bending to study a corpse would not have caused my spine to stiffen. I was accustomed to being young. The approach of mature years has come upon me with little warning. I suppose an aching back might be construed as a notice.

"You find any cause for this death?" Sir Jaket asked as I stood.

"Nay. 'Tis a puzzle. He bears no wounds nor injury but for what the pigs did. Of course, he could have been stabbed in his belly and the hogs destroyed the evidence."

"'Tis sure," Sir Jaket said, "he did not die in the normal course of life and death. Else he would not be here with a thin layer of earth and leaves as cover to his bones."

"Aye. He was surely slain. How, and why, I do not know."

"Poison, mayhap?" Sir Jaket said.

"Possible," I agreed. "But how could he be persuaded to consume the toxin, and who would offer it?"

"His wife. All know he mistreated her."

"Mayhap. But the last meal she prepared for him was a pottage which all of the family consumed. I saw through an open door as Edmund ate from the same kettle as the others."

"Poisoned ale, then?"

I scratched my head, then remembered. "As I departed I saw Leuca refill Edmund's cup and, I think, her own from a leather ewer. If his ale was poisoned, the stuff could not have been in the ewer."

Sir Jaket shrugged. "You're the bailiff. 'Tis your problem, not my own."

"Indeed. We should be away. But we will stop at the castle before taking Edmund to Leuca, and get a shroud."

At that moment Will Shillside and his jury arrived. I and Sir Jaket stood back to allow them to view the corpse, and Thomas told again how he had discovered Edmund. Will and his jury put their heads together briefly, then announced a verdict: willful murder, felon unknown.

The dead man lay face up upon the canvas pallet, his clothing in disarray and his viscera – what remained of it – sickeningly visible. Neither Leuca nor the children should see the repulsive work the pigs had done. At some time, I suppose, Leuca would peel back the shroud. But her first glimpse of her dead husband would be shock enough. She did not need to compound the misery by gazing upon the gory mess that was Edmund's gut.

Leuca said little when Uctred and Squire Thomas set down the pallet bearing Edmund at her door. I saw a tear leak from her eye, but otherwise she showed little emotion when she drew back the shroud and gazed at her husband's face. Decomposition had not yet begun, so he was readily identifiable, though filth encrusted his beard, cheeks, and hair.

Father Thomas was present. He could not ask the seven interrogations of a dead man, but touched Edmund's filthy forehead with fingers dipped in holy water, spoke the paternoster, then backed from the corpse, his obligation completed. For the moment.

A crowd began to gather on Rosemary Lane. Folk had seen Uctred and Squire Thomas carrying a shrouded corpse past the castle and across the bridge over Shill Brook. Word of the peculiar procession had spread quickly.

I did not think it meet that Edmund, or Leuca and her children, should be objects of curiosity for villagers, so told Uctred and Thomas to move Edmund into the house. Leuca stood aside to allow them to pass. The children stood silent, open-mouthed at what they saw and heard.

Onlookers engaged in whispered conversations, then wandered away, leaving me, Leuca, Sir Jaket, and Father Thomas standing awkwardly in the muddy lane.

"I've no money for a wake," Leuca said softly. "Edmund kept 'is coins in a secret place. Wouldn't tell me where."

"You are penniless?" I asked.

"Aye. 'Less I can find where Edmund hid 'is coins."

Edmund and Leuca possessed a two-bay house, a shed, and a hen coop. Somewhere within those three structures Edmund had likely kept what little money a man of his station possessed.

"Said 'e kept 'is money hid so thieves couldn't seize it," Leuca said. "But 'twas me 'e didn't want to 'ave even a farthing."

"We will find the coins," I said. "'Tis your money now. Yours and the lad's," I said, nodding to the elder son. "With your permission we will search house, shed, and hen coop."

Leuca agreed, and I set Sir Jaket to searching the shed, Uctred and Thomas to investigating the hen coop, and Father Thomas and I poked through the house. 'Twas the priest who found the coins. He lifted the hearthstone and under it found a cavity in the soil. From this hole he drew a scorched leather pouch which contained, as best I can remember, three groats, sixteen pennies, five ha'pennies, and nine farthings. Such a hoard did not make Leuca suddenly wealthy, but she would not starve through the winter and spring to come.

The woman held the bag in her hands and what might pass for joy brightened her features.

"Do not squander this on a wake for Edmund," I cautioned. "Your children need the coins more than Edmund now."

Leuca's mouth turned down and I wondered what thought had so changed her countenance. Was it my advice concerning a wake? Nay.

"What 'eriot will Lord Gilbert require?"

Edmund may have kept a sow or two, but I thought it likely they were housed in some other place, along with pigs owned by other tenants, for there was no place in his toft where swine might be kept. It occurred to me that perhaps one of the hogs which had rooted about amongst his bowels had been his own.

"A hen will suffice," I said. I knew this because the decision of a heriot was mine to make.

The wife of Bampton's baker makes good ale, and against my advice Leuca purchased six pence worth to slake the thirst of those who came to her house as night fell. Holy Mother Church frowns on the frivolity and drunkenness such an event incites. To no effect. Men will find cause to celebrate even death, especially because it is the death of another, not their own.

Kate and I fell to sleep with the raucous observance loud in our ears, even through closed windows.

Chapter 3

$\mathfrak{N}$ext morning at the third hour I heard the sound of keening. 'Twas Leuca and Edmund's sister, wailing behind the corpse as Walter and Osbert bore it from Rosemary Lane, past Galen House, to St. Beornwald's Church.

There were few mourners in the procession, for there were few who lamented Edmund's death. I fell in behind Leuca, but Kate refused to join me in the short walk to the churchyard. She did not mourn the knave's passing and would not pretend she did. Neither did I mourn, but I thought I might observe the few who did. Mayhap some clue leading to a killer might appear.

None did.

Leuca had spent another ha'penny to rent a coffin from Philip Carpenter. Walter and Osbert set Edmund down under the lychgate, Father Thomas and Father Ralph spoke the Mourning Office, then Father Thomas led the brief procession to a corner of the churchyard where a fresh-dug grave lay open. The sexton and two clerks pried open the coffin, and using the shroud lifted Edmund from the box to his grave. I was pleased that the man would not await the return of the Lord Christ anywhere near my father-in-law. His grave lay thirty or so paces to the west. What difference the location of Edmund's grave could make to my deceased father-in-law I cannot say. But it made a difference to me.

As I departed the churchyard my gaze traveled the length of Church View Street and I saw mounted men passing the crossing with Bridge Street. Lord Gilbert had returned. I was eager to learn of matters at court, and my employer needed to know of the death of a tenant. Leuca would be responsible for rents payable for the land she now held, but no lord wants to lose tenants. They are difficult to come by since the pestilence.

As I passed under the lychgate I heard my name being called. I turned to see Father Thomas hurrying to me, his robe flapping about bony ankles.

"The replacement for Father Simon arrived late last night. I told him he need not participate in this day's funeral, but he has volunteered to observe the noon Angelus. He is young, is Father Harold. Harold Brantyngham."

"Brantyngham?" I said.

"Aye. The same. The bishop's nephew. Sent to Bampton, his first low rung on the ladder to a bishopric of his own. He will, no doubt, be in frequent communication with his uncle regarding the Church of St. Beornwald."

"Why would the bishop want to have an informer peering over your shoulder?"

"Why, indeed? Mayhap my imagination is too fertile."

"Mayhap," I agreed. "But caution may be the best policy for a few months, to learn which way the wind blows."

Father Thomas was wise, I thought, to view the appointment of this new priest with suspicion. Bampton is not a posting designed to further the ecclesiastical career of a priest with strong family connections. Why, then, was Father Harold sent here? What duty was he assigned? Father Thomas and Father Ralph had served St. Beornwald's Church for decades. They had reached the pinnacle of their theological profession, knew this to be so, and were content. Was Bampton the place where Harold Brantyngham would live out his days serving the Lord Christ and Holy Mother Church? His name made this future unlikely.

Walter and Osbert passed whilst I spoke to Father Thomas, carrying the empty coffin back to Philip Carpenter, where it might be hired out again. Some day a wife or husband with a fatter purse than most may purchase the box and inter their spouse within its wooden walls to await the Lord Christ's return. Did I look upon what might become the repository for my own bones? Would my Kate bury me in a coffin to mark my status in the town, or would a simple shroud be adequate? What would I care then of honor? Do folk in heaven look down upon those who remain? From heaven, mayhap, but surely not from purgatory, if there is such a place.

I must write no more of this matter. Too often I have come near to embracing trouble for my unorthodox view of the afterlife.

Adela was in the toft behind Galen House, standing with a pole over a steaming pot, stirring linen undergarments in the hot water. In summer the heat of such work would be unwelcome, but today the blaze under the pot was pleasant. Kate would want to know who had attended Edmund's funeral. I would tell her later. I continued on my way to the castle and conversation with Lord Gilbert.

There is much to occupy a lord's attention when he returns to his demesne after an absence. I found Lord Gilbert surrounded by grooms, valets, and household knights, each requiring his attention regarding some matter of castle business. And standing near the stairs to the solar were Sir Roger, his wife, and the lovely Rohilda.

Lord Gilbert would be busy for some hours. I did not need much of his time, nor did I need from him a decision or an opinion. I needed only to provide information, and decided the best way to do that was through John Chamberlain. I elbowed my way through the chattering throng to John, told him of my purpose, and asked him to tell Lord Gilbert that I must speak briefly to him. John, by virtue of his position, was able to push through the babbling crowd and gain Lord Gilbert's attention.

My employer and I are taller than most men. I saw Lord Gilbert bend to listen to John Chamberlain's words, then he peered over the heads of the crowd, saw me, and nodded toward the steps to the solar.

At the top of the steps, at the door to the solar, Richard stood and watched his father's return. He also dropped his gaze occasionally to the three guests who stood below him. Rohilda was near his age and worth any young man's second look. Or third.

No man would follow Lord Gilbert up the steps to his private chamber unless invited, so he was able to escape all who demanded his attention by climbing the stairs. Halfway up he stopped, turned to look down upon his retainers, and told them he would make time for all. They must schedule an appointment with John Chamberlain. Then he beckoned to me and I followed him to the solar. I caught a glimpse of Rohilda as I mounted the stairs. The lass was not happy. I believe she was unaccustomed to being overlooked.

"What news, Hugh?" Lord Gilbert asked after John had closed the solar door to the undercurrent of conversation which had followed us up the stairs.

"There has been a death, a murder, since you departed for Prince Edward's funeral. Edmund Harkins was buried this morning."

"Harkins? Is he the lout known for beating his wife?"

"Aye, he was of that reputation." I told my employer of Edmund's disappearance, his discovery in a shallow grave, and also of the arrival of Father Harold Brantyngham.

"Brantyngham?" Lord Gilbert repeated, raising one eyebrow. How does he do that, I wonder? "Related to the bishop, no doubt."

"His nephew," I said.

"Hmm," was his only response.

"I saw Sir Roger in the castle yard," he continued.

"Aye. He arrived yesterday. You invited him to visit, you remember," John reminded him.

"Ah, so I did. Though he rather invited himself. Who are the females accompanying him?"

"His wife, Lady Emma, and daughter Rohilda. The lass, I surmise, is here for your inspection."

"Another one?" Lord Gilbert smiled. "So that's why he wrote telling me he would be passing through Bampton and would be pleased to call."

"Likely," John said.

"Is Leuca able to work her lands?" Lord Gilbert asked me, changing the subject.

"She will have to hire a plow team, but her oldest lad can help with seeding and harvest. She will not starve. And there are two men of your tenancy, and one in the Weald, who have lost wives to childbirth and the pestilence. No doubt they will soon seek her attention. Although after her experience with Edmund she may not welcome suitors."

"Have you suspicions as to who may have slain Edmund? I hope 'twas not another of my tenants or villeins. Laborers are difficult to come by. Losing one is troublesome enough. I'd hate to lose another to the sheriff's gallows."

"With luck," John said, "the guilty man will be a tenant of the Bishop of Exeter in the Weald."

"We may so hope," Lord Gilbert said, then dismissed me with a request to keep him informed.

I departed the solar by means of the outside stairs to the castle yard and saw that Richard was no longer outside the solar door ogling the lass who might be his future stepmother – if Sir Roger had his way. Rohilda and her parents were yet at the base of the stairs, in close conversation, no doubt hoping Lord Gilbert would soon appear above them and invite them to join him. Whether or not this happened I know not. I departed for Galen House and sought my dinner.

A simple pottage of peas, beans, and leeks awaited me. 'Twas not a meal over which to linger, savoring each morsel. And I wished to visit the holy man. His practice of prowling Bampton's streets after curfew might mean that he saw some men about in the night when Edmund vanished. Men who might have to do with Harkins' death. As I departed Galen House the noon Angelus rang from St. Beornwald's tower.

The holy man was dozing upon his pallet when I approached his modest dwelling. The door was open to a mild breeze, a pot cooled over ashes on the hearthstone, and the holy man snored softly. A man who spends much of the night awake must sleep at some time. A full belly will invite Morpheus to visit most men. Even me, and I sleep the night through.

I rapped softly upon the open door, so as not to startle the fellow. He stirred, then rubbed his eyes and propped himself up on an elbow. The light from the open door was behind me, my face and form but a shadow to the holy man. I realized this and announced my presence so as not to alarm him.

He climbed shakily to his feet, as men do when awakened from slumber. The man could not ask the reason for my appearance, so I spoke. I pointed to a bench in the shadows below a skin window, asked him to sit, and sat myself at the opposite end of the bench.

"The man Thomas Neckham found in the shallow grave had been missing for several days," I began.

The holy man nodded understanding.

"From Monday to Friday did you roam Bampton's streets in the night?"

The holy man nodded.

"How many nights? One? Or all?"

The fellow raised two fingers.

"Which two nights? Monday?"

He shook his head.

"Tuesday?"

Again he shook his head.

"Wednesday and Thursday, then?"

I was taken aback when he again shook his head.

"Wednesday?" I asked.

He nodded.

"But not Thursday night?"

He shook his head.

"That is but one night. When was the second? Ah. . . Sunday night?"

The holy man nodded.

"Did you see other men about after curfew on either of these nights?"

Again a nod.

"Sunday night?"

Another nod.

"Wednesday night?"

He shook his head.

"Take me to the place where on Sunday night you saw men."

The holy man stood, beckoned with a finger, and led me from his hut. He touched the ashes on his hearthstone to be sure they were cool, then carefully closed the door behind him and set out for the road to Cowley's Corner, which is but forty or so paces from his dwelling.

He led me past the castle, across the bridge over Shill Brook, thence to a place where Church View Street meets Bridge Street. Here was a copse of black mulberry bushes. Their fruit was long since harvested and the foliage nearly gone. The bare branches would not hide a man in the day, but at night a man garbed in a dark cotehardie would be invisible to any who passed by.

The holy man pushed the branches aside and motioned for me to follow. I found myself in the midst of the copse, looking out toward the length of Church View Street.

"Here is where you saw men Sunday night?" I asked.

He nodded.

"Before midnight?"

A shake of the head.

"After midnight?"

A nod.

"Near to dawn?"

He nodded again.

"So in the dark of the night, before dawn Monday, you saw men pass by this place?"

Another nod.

"How many?"

The holy man shrugged and raised three fingers, then four, then five.

"You are unsure how many men you saw in the dark?"

He nodded.

Here was no surprise. There had been no moon Sunday night, and clouds obscured even starlight. The night would have been as black as a carrion crow.

"Show me now where these men first appeared, and the path they traveled."

We departed the copse and I followed the holy man east on Bridge Street to where Rosemary Lane entered the larger thoroughfare.

"Here is where this group first appeared?"

He nodded.

"Show me where they went."

The holy man led me west, across the bridge over Shill Brook, and I convinced myself that he would lead me past the castle to the forest.

"Did these men carry any object?" I asked.

He shrugged again, then raised his palms in an expression of ignorance. Indeed, so dark would have been the night 'twas a wonder he saw anything at all. If the men the holy man saw carried a corpse, the night was too black for him to see.

We came to the lane leading to the Weald and here the holy man turned aside.

"The men you saw Sunday night traveled to the Weald?" I said incredulously. If they had to do with Edmund's death why take him there – dead or alive? And how then transport his corpse to a hidden place in a wood? Nothing made sense. Not to me. All is clear to the Lord Christ, however, and if I cannot uncover the truth of Edmund's death in this life the Lord Christ will explain all in the next. But I would rather not wait 'til then for resolution of the matter.

"Did you follow the men to the Weald?" I asked.

He nodded.

"To which house did they go?"

Another shrug.

"Did you lose sight of them in the dark?"

A nod.

"What then? Did you return to your hut?"

Another nod.

"As you lay upon your pallet for the remainder of Sunday night, did you hear any sound, as of men stumbling through a dark wood?"

The holy man shook his head.

If the men he saw Sunday night slew Edmund Harkins they did not bury him that same night. The forest would have been so dark they could not have entered it silently. They would have stumbled over roots and fallen branches. Even brittle leaves would have told their passage. But certainly Edmund was buried in the night, not the day. Monday or Tuesday night, mayhap. Was the corpse hidden someplace in the Weald for a day or two?

A sliver of crescent moon would have provided a little light shortly after sunset Tuesday or Wednesday evening. Mayhap one of those nights Edmund was buried in the forest. The holy man had prowled Bampton's streets Wednesday evening, but seen no men about. Did men visit the wood at a time when the holy man was not near? Would they know of his occasional nocturnal absence from the forest surrounding his abode?

The holy man's night-time activity is not generally known, I believe, but that is not to say that all men of Bampton or the Weald are ignorant of his custom. Perhaps they set a lookout to watch his hut, and when he was seen to depart they brought Edmund's corpse to the wood, secure in the knowledge that they would not be heard or seen as they dug a shallow grave.

The holy man could tell me little more. I dismissed him and watched as he walked past the castle. I turned then to Rosemary Lane. I needed to speak again to Leuca Harkins. How could Edmund have departed his house in the night and roused no other? More to the point, could he have been taken from his house silently by men who intended him harm?

Mayhap, if he did not know their purpose.

Leuca was not home. I found her near to St. Andrew's Chapel, east of the town, planting rye on strips which were now hers, if she could meet the rent next Michaelmas. Her children attended her, the babe playing with a stick at the edge of the field, the two older children breaking clods with their feet as Leuca scattered the seed. She had buried her husband only six hours earlier, but life must go on.

The woman did not work alone. Other of Lord Gilbert's tenants toiled at similar tasks in their own strips, and just beyond St. Andrew's Chapel a plow team was about to finish turning the sod of the last autumn plowing.

'Twas twilight, and would soon be night. I did not enter the strip, for I knew that as darkness approached, Leuca would cease her work and seek her home. Then would be opportunity to speak to her. She knew I stood at the edge of the field, for I saw her glance several times in my direction. But she did not cease her labor and greet me until the strip was sown and darkness near.

"Good eve, Sir Hugh. Do you wish to inspect my wound? 'Tis nearly healed, I think. Will you remove the stitches soon? The cut sometimes itches, but I feel no pain." The woman spoke rapidly, as if she wanted to set the conversation before I could speak.

"I'll walk with you to Rosemary Lane. Mayhap you can settle a matter for me. Your husband was found yesterday in a shallow grave. Was he living when he crept from your house last Sunday night, or was he slain whilst you slept? What think you?"

"Slain while I slept? Nay. Such a thing would surely rouse me. 'E must 'ave been drawn away. Mayhap 'e 'eard somethin' in the night an' went out to see what 'twas."

"Mayhap." Such a suggestion was as good a theory as any I had considered. What could draw a man from the warmth of his bed and the safety of his house, the door being barred, in the middle of the night?

If the holy man was to be believed, and there was no reason he should not, several men were about on Bampton streets the night Edmund vanished. Was he one of these? Was he their captive? Did he walk to the Weald of his own volition, or was he forced to go there? Or slain when outside his house and carried to the Weald a corpse?

Darkness was upon the town when I departed Rosemary Lane. I resolved that the following day, after mass, I would walk the length of the Weald. What did I seek? Anything suspicious, I suppose. Perhaps some man would watch me through a cracked-open door as I passed, his secretive gaze betraying guilt.

Chapter 4

The new vicar, Father Harold, spoke the homily Sunday morning. His message was brief but clear. Men must obey the dictates of Holy Mother Church. To question its teachings was heresy, and the bishops, to whom the Lord Christ in His wisdom had given the administration of His kingdom on earth, were resolved to deal firmly with heretics and root out all false teaching. Could anyone doubt, he concluded, that the returning pestilence indicated the Lord Christ's anger against sinful men? The only way to escape His wrath was to carefully observe the bishops' teaching.

My Kate, knowing my views, glanced toward me several times from the corner of her eye. No doubt she would prefer that I not become an excommunicant, liable to be attacked and slain by any man, unable to find employment or care for my family. Did the priest look in my direction whilst he spoke? Or did my conscience see what was not?

Father Thomas and Father Ralph sat stone-faced as Father Harold spoke. I suspect they heard in his homily a veiled charge that they had been lax in disciplining their parish. A new priest of twenty or so years should not have the audacity to lecture his elders. Now that I am no longer youthful I feel the validity of this assertion.

I was sure, however, that Father Thomas and Father Ralph would not openly object to Father Harold's effrontery. He was the bishop's nephew. Did he speak what his uncle had demanded, or did he hope his words would eventually be spoken of in the bishop's palace and earn him plaudits and promotion?

Dinner was a quiet meal but for John smacking his lips and Bessie's enthusiasm for life. Kate and I had little to say – not in front of Adela and Bessie. Neither I nor my spouse wanted my views of purgatory known to either servant or daughter and carelessly repeated. Father Thomas and Father Ralph suspect, I believe, that I do not hold with the doctrine because I find no justification for it in Scripture. Perhaps they silently agree with me. But clearly Father Harold would not. Fortunately, no one in Bampton is likely to ask my view on the subject, so I will not be required to prevaricate.

When dawn had broken that Sunday morning Adela placed a capon upon the spit. The scent had traveled up the stairs and roused me pleasantly from slumber. Kate, as is her custom, was already up and about. I drew on my cotehardie and as I did I heard someone retching in the toft. I am a surgeon, not a physician, but I decided that after dinner I must interrogate Kate about her condition. If she was ill, I might have herbs which could alleviate her distress.

"Do you not remember," she smiled in response to my inquiry, "when I last was suffering thusly?"

I did. "You are with child?"

"Indeed. My indisposition is common to women in the first month or so. 'Twill soon pass. It always does."

This was so. I remembered that when Kate bore Bessie and Sybil and John, she cleaned her trencher and would have more. I sighed with relief that her malady was curable. Time and birth would work the remedy.

I set out to walk the Weald with a lighter heart. Solomon wrote that children are like arrows. Happy is the man who has a quiver full. He was silent about the delights of the wife whose work it was to fill the quiver.

Smoke drifted from vent holes as wives of Bampton and the Weald prepared their families' dinners. Galen House is one of the few in the town equipped with a hearth, fireplace, and chimney. A few inhabitants of the Weald glanced my way as I walked their lane. All knew who I was, and no doubt wondered what business Lord Gilbert's bailiff had in the Bishop of Exeter's demesne.

One of the houses along the path had received the shadowy figures the holy man had seen Sunday night. He could not tell me which one, for he had lost their trail when they turned from Bridge Street. More's the pity. There are twelve dwellings in the Weald. One of these held a secret I sought to discover. But I had no way to learn which one. After arousing the curiosity of some of the inhabitants, I departed the Weald.

At Bridge Street I met Adela. Kate had released her from her duties and she was on her way to her parents' home in the Weald. I greeted the lass as we passed. She replied with a fleeting smile and hurried on.

Clouds had obscured the sun since noon, and a cold mist began to fall as I approached Galen House. I had no desire to pursue a murderer if the work would take me from my hearth and leave me soaked. I spent the remainder of the day sitting on a bench, my Bible opened before me, and read from it to Kate. My wife has no Latin, so I translated as I read. Would Father Harold consider this a violation of the bishops' command that the Bible not be rendered in the common tongue? Surely not. But then, a bishop's decision is not always predictable. Neither are the thoughts of a bishop's lackey. I resolved not to ask Father Harold of his opinion.

I read from the book of Proverbs. Its wisdom is always valuable. I came to a verse which read, "It is joy to the just to do judgment: but destruction shall be to the workers of iniquity."

"Is that you?" Kate asked. "Do you find it a joy to seek justice? Do you take pleasure in bringing destruction to workers of iniquity?"

"I probably should not, for we are told we must love mercy. Yet I admit I am happy when I charge a villain with his crime."

I was breaking my fast Monday morning with a maslin loaf and ale when Adela arrived. Kate was yet abed, for I had demanded of her that, as her nausea was greatest early in the day, she remain abed 'til the sun was well up. She did not resist this admonition.

Adela entered the kitchen, saw me, and stammered that I must come with her. She led me to my front door, a stout portal of thick oaken planks equipped with iron latch, hinges, and a lock. In the night I kept it barred against intruders. I had only moments before unbarred the door in expectation that Adela would soon arrive.

Who would enter a bailiff's house in the night? There is little profit in robbing the poor, but bailiffs are generally not. Their reputation is that of men who steal from their employer and extort fines and rents. I am not such a man, but there are those who may believe me to be so. Hence my robust door. And the kitchen door is much the same.

Adela drew back the door, stepped aside, and pointed. She could not read, so did not know what was inscribed in scratches upon the oak.

Gouged into the door, in letters nearly unintelligible, was "leav itt bee". Whoso had written the words was literate, but barely. What was I to "leav bee"? What was I doing which some man wished me not to do? I sought the man or men who slew Edmund Harkins. Nothing else that I was about would cause a man to advise me to cease. Perhaps the vandal was frightened away before he could inscribe a warning or threat. Certainly there was the implication that if I continued to seek Edmund's murderer I would cause some man great anger. I have made miscreants angry before, and bear scars to prove their wrath. Would some day Kate be a widow because I sought malefactors? Such is always dangerous work.

A man can easily find excuses to escape an onerous duty. Potential pain and death are amongst the most effective of these. I admit that consideration of such deplorable possibilities crossed my mind. But I have been accused of stubbornness. Often by Kate.

Kate! I would not have her see the warning scratched into our door. A woman with child has enough to worry her. I went to the rear of Galen House and in the toft found a flat stone about the circumference of my fist. Then quietly, so as not to rouse Kate, I used the stone to polish away the words defacing my door. The work took only a few minutes. When the task was finished, only a lighter patch on the weathered oak showed where the message had been worn away.

Adela had been watching silently as I expunged the words. When I was satisfied that the message was fully obliterated I spoke to her.

"Do not tell your mistress of what you found here, nor of what I have done," I said.

The lass nodded. I'm sure she understood the reason for this admonition.

The words found on my door were likely inscribed with the point of a dagger. All men of Bampton and the Weald own such a weapon. But not all men who possess a dagger go about with it in the dark of night intending mischief.

Kate came down the stairs as I finished breaking my fast. She glanced at the remaining half-loaf and a look of revulsion briefly darkened her face. Clearly her appetite had not yet returned. She turned her back to the fire and spoke to Adela about preparing our dinner. While she looked away I caught Adela's eye and put a finger to my lips. The lass nodded imperceptibly.

I would enjoy chicken in bruit for my dinner, after I returned from again visiting the holy man. Mayhap, I thought, he had been upon Bampton's streets in the night and saw the man who defaced my door. I told Kate where I was going, but not the reason for my visit, and that I would return for my dinner. Then, with a last inspection of Galen House door, I set off for the holy man's hut.

A man who prowls the town in the night is likely to sleep late. I rapped upon the holy man's door twice before he opened to me, rubbing his eyes and appearing peeved to be awakened. Nevertheless, he signaled me to enter.

I did not tell him of the words carved into my door. I did suggest that someone had been about after curfew and asked if in his tenebrous meandering he had seen anyone near to Church View Street. He shook his head.

"Were you upon the streets last night?"

He nodded.

"But you saw no man?"

He shook his head nay.

If a man knew that the holy man is oft upon Bampton's streets in the night he might watch for him and, knowing where he was and where he was not, choose a time to approach Galen House when the holy man was somewhere else.

I bade the holy man good day and walked past the castle and Galen House to Laundels Lane, where John Whitestaff, the town's newly chosen beadle, resides. 'Tis John's duty to see that all men are off the streets at curfew, or, if they are not, they have with them a lantern and a good reason they are not at home.

John knows of the holy man's nocturnal practice. Indeed, I told him when he assumed the office that he might occasionally see the fellow, and if he did, he was not to admonish him. As John's work ended an hour or so after nightfall, and the holy man did not usually leave his hut 'til midnight, they seldom met.

I thought it doubtful that the man who had marred Galen House door would have done so immediately after dark, when he knew the beadle might be upon his rounds. But John should be asked if he had challenged anyone the previous night. He had not.

As with the holy man, I did not tell the beadle of the damage to my door, but charged him to be especially vigilant for the next week or so, as I had reason to believe a man or men might be upon the streets in violation of curfew. John nodded agreement and did not ask why I had voiced the suspicion. Bailiffs, he likely thought, were strange fellows who may be relied upon to make occasional obscure demands.

Kate understood my concern for her lack of appetite, so struggled to choke down a reasonable portion of chicken in bruit and thus allay my apprehension. Bessie, as usual, chattered about one thing after another, whilst John, also as usual, concentrated on filling his mouth to its utmost capacity.

When dinner was over I summoned Adela to the hall, a room she seldom had cause to visit. She would know I had a weighty matter to discuss, because of the rare invitation. She resided with her parents in the Weald, and the holy man had seen men in the darkest hour of night pass from Rosemary Lane to the Weald.

I motioned to a bench, sat in a chair opposite, and sensed Adela's discomfort. Why was she ill at ease? Was it due to being in a part of Galen House she seldom entered, or because she knew something of the murder which now consumed my time and wished not to speak of it?

"Men were seen," I began, "a week past, late Sunday night, walking from Bridge Street into the Weald. The man who saw them lost sight of them. 'Twas a moonless night. Have you, in the past week, heard gossip of folk being about in the Weald after curfew?"

John Whitestaff's obligation does not include the Weald, and the vicars of St. Beornwald's Church have not seen fit to assign a man to patrol the place for curfew violators.

"Nay, sir," she replied.

"Holy Writ says men love darkness rather than light because their deeds are evil. So the men seen last Sunday night were surely about some evil. If they were doing a thing of which other men approve they would have done it in the day."

Adela is a shy lass, and often avoids looking me in the eye when spoken to. But as I spoke I thought her reticence greater even than usual. She glanced about the hall as if seeing it for the first time. Not once did she meet my gaze.

Bailiffs are a skeptical sort. Folk we deal with provide us reason to be. I was suspicious that Adela knew more about midnight activity in the Weald than she wanted to speak of. But how to pry the information from her? I could threaten to end her employment if she would not tell what she knew.

It would be an empty threat, for I would do no such thing. The lass is a great help to Kate, and I rue the day some lad will claim Adela as wife. And mayhap she really was unaware of night-time activity in the Weald. The fact that occasionally folk may be innocent is another truth bailiffs find difficult to accept. 'Tis our nature.

And Kate would be furious if I discharged her. When my Kate is happy, I am happy. Adela likely knows this, so would understand that any threat I made to end her labor at Galen House would be hollow. Bailiffs should not be known in their manor for making idle threats. If they do so they will lose a potent weapon against malefactors.

"If you hear folk of the Weald speak of men going about after curfew, or talking of Edmund Harkins' murder, tell me or your mistress at once." I said this with an edge to my voice. The words were no threat, but the tone was. Adela knew it to be so.

"Aye, sir," she replied with a quavering voice.

I sent the lass back to Kate and as she departed I heard a rapping upon Galen House door. I opened to find Father Thomas.

"I give you good day, Father," I greeted the priest. "How may I serve you?"

"'Tis I who may be of service to you," he replied. My first thought was that he had learned something which might put me on the track of whoso slew Edmund Harkins.

"Come in," I said, and directed him to the hall whence Adela had just departed. I pointed to the bench, but this time, rather than seat myself upon a chair opposite him, I sat at the other end of the bench. "What service might you perform for me?" I asked. I knew that he could not repeat what he had heard in the confessional, even if a murderer might escape punishment because of his silence, but thought he might have gained information in some other way.

'Twas information I certainly found valuable, but it had naught to do with murder.

"Father Harold is an inquisitive man," the priest began. "In the days he has been here he has voiced many questions about the town and its inhabitants. Especially you."

"Me?" I said stupidly.

"Aye. Several folk have come to me in the past few days asking why the new priest is so curious about Sir Hugh."

"Who?"

"This morning John Kellet visited me."

Kellet is the priest at St. Andrew's Chapel, a tiny parish to the east of Bampton. The fellow was once slovenly and obese, but I caught him in league with a man who poached Lord Gilbert's deer. For this transgression the bishop required that he go on pilgrimage to Compostela. Kellet returned five stone lighter, emaciated. The man now goes barefoot in all weather, wears a threadbare robe, has a rosary made of acorns suspended on a hempen string, and gives all he possesses to the poor. Seldom has pilgrimage so changed a man.

"What did Father Harold want to know that he thought John Kellet could tell him?"

"He learned from someone that Kellet holds your views of purgatory."

"Does he? And what are my views of purgatory?"

"Do not be disingenuous. All of Bampton – well, nearly all – know that you doubt the existence of the place."

How could this be? 'Twas true enough, but I had been careful to keep my views to myself. Most of the time.

"I believe of purgatory only what is said of the place in Scripture," I said.

Father Thomas was silent for a moment. "What is that?" he finally asked. "You have me there."

"Nothing. Holy Writ says nothing of a place of torment where men must endure years of suffering to erase their sins."

"But does it say there is not such a place? If 'tis silent then mayhap there is."

"Would the Lord Christ and His saints be mute about such a troubling place which awaits all men? Would St. Paul have forgotten to mention it in his letters to the churches? He warned the early believers of many things, but never of purgatory. In the letter to the Hebrews the writer says that 'tis given to men once to die, and then the judgment. No mention of purgatory between the two."

"But the bishops insist there is such a place."

"Aye, they have done so for many years," I replied. "The teaching has brought them much wealth."

"You believe that is why Holy Mother Church holds that purgatory exists?"

"What does Scripture say about a rich man entering heaven?" I replied.

"'Twill not be easy," Father Thomas said grudgingly.

"Aye. But the bishops say that if a wealthy man gives coins and lands to the church, priests and monks will pray him out of purgatory sooner than his sins would otherwise allow. But the poor man, who has no lands or chattels with which to enrich the bishops, will languish in purgatory for a thousand years. Mayhap more."

"Mayhap if a man is poor 'tis because of his sins."

"Perhaps," I agreed. "But more likely he chose the wrong father."

"Hmm – aye," the priest chuckled.

"You came here to warn me," I said, "and for that, much thanks. Do you suppose Father Harold was sent here because word of my views has traveled all the way to Exeter and the bishop's palace?"

"Such could be. Father Ralph and I have puzzled over why a bishop's nephew would be sent to Bampton. Perhaps to spy out heresy."

"My heresy? Or are there other heretics lurking about the town?"

"Sinners, there are plenty. Heretics, I know not. Nor do I wish to know."

"I thank you," I said, "for this caution. I will be circumspect."

"'Twould be wise. If you are accused of unorthodox views, Father Ralph and I will be admonished for allowing your opinions to flourish."

"But you have not... allowed my views to flourish."

"Will that make any difference to an offended bishop?"

"Probably not," I said.

"On another matter, how goes your search for a murderer?"

"Not well. And don't appear so agreeable."

"I told you some days past that I could feel no sorrow for Edmund Harkins' death. The town has one less sinner."

"And if plague strikes again and sends us all to the churchyard," I said, "there will be no sinners in Bampton at all. Wherever men reside there is also sin."

"True enough, as any priest knows well. And although I have no regret that such as Edmund is dead, I will keep my ear to the ground and tell you of any gossip I hear which might be of use to you."

"Much thanks."

I showed Father Thomas to the door and when he stepped over the threshold he stopped to study the planks. It was clear that someone had scoured away some blemish. Did the priest need to know what had been inscribed there? Probably not, but I decided to tell him anyway.

"A message was left here during the night," I said. "Some man scratched 'leave it be' upon my door. I have rubbed it away."

"Hmm. What are you to leave be?" the priest asked.

"The search for a murderer, I believe. I am not engaged in any other business a man would want me to quit, I think."

"There was no threat included?"

"Nay."

"Nevertheless, you should watch your back. The bishop's nephew seeks you harm, I believe, and some man of the town objects to your search for a murderer. A man who attempts to do good can make many enemies."

"A bailiff makes many enemies. The important thing is that they be the proper enemies. 'Do good'? Then you agree with me about purgatory?"

"Did I say so? I will say only that I do not intend to preach a homily upon the subject. Now, I give you good day."

And with that the priest turned and walked away. He had given me much to consider.

And Kate also. As I closed the door behind the priest my wife appeared. She was not pleased. She had heard the conversation from beyond the door from hall to kitchen.

"You did not tell me that a message was left upon our door," she said.

"You slept and I saw no cause to wake you."

"No cause? A threat is a cause."

"There was no threat," I replied. "'Twas a request."

"A request that you cease the search for a murderer? Who would request such a thing? 'Twas a command, I fear, and folk who would be so bold as to command their bailiff intend to intimidate."

"They have failed."

"Not completely. They have intimidated the bailiff's wife. And so has the new vicar. I have wondered at his interest. Now I understand."

"His interest? In what?"

"Galen House. Thrice I have seen him walk past and study Galen House whilst you were away."

"You did not tell me."

"You did not tell me of the door. Many men walk Church View Street. 'Twas only after I heard Father Thomas speak that I understood Father Harold's curiosity. Do be careful. What might an angry bishop do?"

"I prefer not to think on it," I said.

"Nor I."

"If it is possible to avoid a bishop's wrath you may trust me to do so."

"But I know my husband. You prefer truth to comfort."

"I am not opposed to comfort. I choose it whenever I may."

"Nevertheless, I fear your nature. You believe compromise a character flaw."

"Not all compromise," I protested. "But compromise with evil, aye. You have me there."

Adela appeared at the kitchen door. "The capon is plucked and cleaned," she said.

"Very well," Kate replied. "You may go."

"Thank you, m'lady."

I have been "Sir Hugh" for several years, but it still seems odd to hear my Kate addressed as "Lady Katherine". She is also slow to become accustomed to the title, I think. 'Tis not an appellation either of us expected to have.

"The capon is for your dinner tomorrow," Kate said.

"Adela's work is done for the day?" I asked.

"Aye. She has asked to be permitted to return to the Weald before dark. . . now that the days grow short."

"Has she spoken of some fear, some danger which worries her?"

"Nay, but any young lass might dread walking dark streets, even with a competent bailiff and beadle at their work."

This was true enough. A lass accosted upon the streets might scream if she could, but those who came to her aid would not find her assailant waiting to be apprehended. If 'twas dark enough she might not recognize the man who set upon her, and even if she did the scoundrel could claim innocence and 'twould be her word against his.

Father Thomas had told me that Father Harold interrogated John Kellet. I decided I should also, so I set off to see him. 'Twould be helpful to know what questions the new vicar had asked and what Kellet had replied.

Kellet has no Latin, so when questioned about purgatory he could claim ignorance of the Scriptures. This, he told me, is what he did. Father Harold demanded he renounce opinions which the bishops condemned, and this Kellet was pleased to do. I could not blame him. The emaciated priest said he told Father Harold that my views were, so far as he knew, also orthodox. I thanked Kellet for his time and set off for home.

Twilight was turning the town gray by the time our conversation ended. 'Twas dark enough that when a black-garbed figure appeared as I came to Galen House I did not recognize the man. And he did not take notice of me, I think, until he was but a few paces away.

'Twas Father Harold, and another reason for his ignorance of my approach was that he studied the shadowy shape of Galen House whilst he slowly sauntered past.

I greeted the priest and he, with a jerk, recognized me and uttered a reply. We continued our opposite ways, he toward Bridge Street, me to Galen House. At my door it occurred to me that Father Harold was walking from his vicarage at a time of day when most men sought home and hearth. Was there some occasion this evening which required a priest? If so, perhaps a bailiff should know of it.

I turned from Galen House to follow Father Harold, who was now nearly a hundred paces distant. The gathering darkness and his determined pace combined to allow me to follow unobserved.

The vicar crossed Shill Brook without once glancing over his shoulder to learn if he was followed. A few paces beyond the bridge he turned to the path leading to the Weald. This was not unexpected. The Weald is of the Bishop of Exeter's properties and being the bishop's nephew he perhaps had some business there. But so near to curfew?

The priest suddenly disappeared. One moment he was a shadowy shape before me, the next he had vanished. Had he entered some house along the way and I had not seen? Nay. No dwelling abutted the lane at the place he was when he faded from view. A copse of shrubbery and coppiced beech trees came near the path.

I stopped in my tracks and sidled to the verge where, if the priest was looking behind him, I might blend with the dark. Had he seen or heard me following? If he had, I must think of an excuse for doing so. The man was already ill disposed toward me. I did not wish to give him another reason to dislike me.

I stood silent, unmoving, listening, watching. I neither saw nor heard anything. Father Harold was gone like a vapor dispersed by the wind. After a few moments I cautiously retreated toward Mill Street. Where the priest had gone and why he had gone there I could not guess. I had other matters to concern me. I would not trouble myself with the curious behavior of the new vicar.

Chapter 5

Tuesday dawned cloudy and misty. Autumn in Britain. Should I have expected warmth and sun? Not so long as the Scots insist upon sending their weather south. I warmed myself at the hearth and consumed a maslin loaf which had not yet gone stale but was at some halfway point between youth and dotage.

That they broke their fast with bread no longer fresh did not trouble Bessie or John. John is not inclined to interrupt his meals with conversation, but Bessie will put voice to her thoughts from the time she awakens until she lays her head upon a pillow at night. I had to remonstrate with her that she must not speak with her mouth full.

Adela had already put the capon to roasting when Kate appeared. My wife took a few bites of maslin loaf, likely because she knew I would protest did she not, and swallowed a cup of watered ale.

"What will you do this day to seek a murderer?" Kate asked.

What I would do and what I was prepared to say before Adela and Bessie were two different things. Adela is of the Weald, where the holy man had last seen men in the night who had likely seized Edmund Harkins. Would she speak of my plans to her father? Mayhap he was one of those who had taken Harkins. Could I trust Adela to keep silence? Bailiffs learn to apportion trust as if it were a commodity as valuable as a sack of groats.

I said something about seeking the holy man in reply to Kate's question, finished my ale, and departed my house. But not to seek the holy man. I walked north, to Father Thomas's vicarage.

His clerk opened to my knock and a moment later the priest, hearing my voice, appeared. I had caught him breaking his fast, his cheeks plump with a partly consumed loaf.

"Good day, Sir Hugh," he said whilst licking his lips. "How may I serve you?"

Clerks, like servants, are known for exchanging gossip. The actions and foibles of their employers are chief among these conversations. What I had to say to Father Thomas I did not want his clerk to hear and then pass on to Father Harold's clerk and thence to the new vicar himself.

"Walk with me," I said. Father Thomas is no dolt. He glanced to his clerk, nodded, and told me to wait while he fetched his cloak. We strolled past Father Harold's vicarage and when we reached Laundels Lane I told Father Thomas of the new vicar's visit to the Weald.

"Is one of the bishop's tenants ill?" I asked. "Father Harold's clerk did not accompany him, so I doubt he went to some house to offer Extreme Unction to a dying man."

"The bishop's tenants are well. . . so far as I know. A few are frail, but none has perished since Maud Priddle died in August."

"So what business, I wonder, did Father Harold have which took him to the Weald when 'twas so near to dark?"

"Why are you so curious?"

I reminded the priest that the holy man had seen men enter the lane to the Weald well past midnight the night Edmund Harkins had vanished.

"You think Father Harold had to do with Harkins' murder?" the priest scoffed. "You see wickedness wherever you look. 'Tis common in men of your position, I think."

"And yours. But until I know why men prowled the Weald after curfew at the time Edmund disappeared, I will be interested in any strange events in the place. And you must admit Father Harold's visit there so late in the day was strange."

"Why must I admit that? Perhaps since I told you of Father Harold's interest in your views of church teachings you seek a way to have him sent from Bampton."

The thought had not crossed my mind, but Father Thomas's assertion was not disagreeable.

"And what of you and Father Ralph? Are you pleased with your new associate? Do not answer. A priest should not tell a falsehood."

The mist, which had been so light as to barely dampen my cloak, became rain. Father Thomas pulled the hood of his cloak over his head and we hurriedly retraced our steps to his vicarage.

I enjoyed rather more than my share of the roasted capon for my dinner. John enthusiastically attacked a drumstick and I could see a time not far off when one capon would not suffice to satisfy my household.

Ten days had passed since I stitched Leuca Harkins' lacerated eyebrow closed. After dinner I donned my damp cloak and walked to Rosemary Lane. Given the precipitation I thought I would find the woman at home. I did.

I prefer to wait two weeks after closing a wound before I remove the sutures, but I have noticed that the sooner the silk threads are removed the less noticeable the scar. Unless, of course, the stitches are removed too soon and the wound reopens.

A smokey fire warmed Leuca's house. Her children were clustered about the hearthstone, fighting off the chill and consuming a dinner of pottage of some sort. Peas, likely, for the color.

"Good day, Sir Hugh," Leuca greeted me cheerfully. The day was cloudy and damp, her husband recently buried, yet the woman seemed light-hearted. Perhaps the realization that she must no longer fear blows from Edmund was compensation for the doleful weather and the absence of a spouse.

Leuca's cut was now a thin pink line above her brow. Where the silk thread punctured the skin were small red dots, but no pus was visible. The wound had healed well and would continue to fade so that within a few months 'twould be nearly invisible to the widowed suitors who would likely be found on Rosemary Lane.

"I have come to inspect your cut and remove the stitches. Be careful not to fall against a bench for a few more days, else the wound may reopen."

The sarcasm seemed lost on Leuca. She stared blandly at me and said nothing.

With my smallest scalpel I cut the threads binding her wound, then with a small bronze tweezer I drew the loose ends. A few tiny dots of blood appeared. I mopped them away with a fragment of linen, and saw no more blood.

"Edmund promised to pay tuppence, did 'e not?" the woman said.

"Aye."

"A moment, please."

Leuca went to a wicker box which rested upon a table, unfastened the lid, and returned with two coins. For which I thanked her. I might have forgiven the debt, but I had done Leuca more than tuppence worth of service. And if word traveled the village that Sir Hugh will perform surgeries gratis I might never again be paid for my skills.

I bade Leuca good day, and as I departed was pleased to see that the rain had ceased. I wound my way through and past the puddles on Church View Street, entered Galen House, and was delighted to find Kate in the kitchen, munching upon a slice of maslin loaf which she had coated with a layer of parsley butter.

Kate saw the startled look in my eyes and spoke. "My appetite is returning," she smiled. "But not yet before noon. How did you find Leuca?"

"I went to Rosemary Lane and there she was."

Kate rolled her eyes. "You know my meaning."

"She is well. Her wound is healing properly."

"And her spirits?"

"The dolor which once greeted folk when they entered Rosemary Lane is gone. Leuca seems content. Even the children smiled at me."

"No doubt Edmund beat them as well as Leuca when they displeased him," Kate said.

"No doubt. Much in that house was lost, but much gained."

"Which, I wonder, does Leuca consider the greater?" Kate mused. "The loss or the gain?"

I have discovered over the past years that when I don't know what to do next, the best thing is to do nothing. I had no good ideas of what I might do to find Edmund Harkins' slayer, so sought other ways to spend the afternoon.

My smallest scalpel was becoming dull. I learned this whilst cutting away Leuca's stitches, so I spent an hour with a whetstone, putting a keen edge on the three blades I possessed. If I could afford better scalpels, made of Toledo steel, I would not need to spend time so often sharpening the instruments.

But sharpening a scalpel is the work of fingers more than the mind, so whilst I worked I pondered the puzzle of Edmund Harkins' death. I had queried the holy man, Leuca, and Thomas Neckham. And required of Adela that she immediately inform me of any loose talk in the Weald about men who broke curfew the night Harkins disappeared. What might I do next? Who might I question? No fresh path appeared before me. The only thing I received from my time with scalpels and whetstone was a scratched finger from testing an edge, and a stint of mild exercise.

My post as Bampton's bailiff causes me to be drawn into many tales of murder and mayhem, and it is my practice to write them down. I had yet two gatherings of parchment left over from the last account I had written, and a small stoppered pot of ink. If I needed more parchment I would have to travel to Oxford, but my Kate could supply more ink.

When I first laid eyes on her – and 'twas a pleasant place for eyes to rest – Kate was assisting her father at his stationer's shop in Oxford. She prepared the oak gall ink he sold to scholars and copyists. So when more ink was required she insisted that I permit her to make it, rather than spend coins unnecessarily. Frugal, my Kate.

Writing down the events of a felony investigation has often helped me clear my mind so as to better concentrate on the facts at hand. I placed a sheet of parchment before me and began writing of the tale you are now reading. Whomever you may be.

Occasionally when I put words to parchment the exercise produces no benefit. This was one of those times. I filled three sheets of parchment with tiny script before the light began to fail and Kate wanted the table for our supper. Adela had prepared arbolettys before she departed for her home in the Weald. I consumed my meal as empty of theories regarding Edmund Harkins' death as before I set pen to parchment.

Wednesday is a fast day, so my morning loaf had no butter. But Adela had visited the baker so at least 'twas fresh. With no plan for the day I decided to visit the castle. I was curious about Lord Gilbert's thoughts concerning the fair Rohilda, and he should know of my failure to identify a murderer. This was not news he would be pleased to hear, nor would I be pleased to tell it. Even less so because I would have to admit that I had no suspects but for shadowy figures who disappeared in the Weald the same time Edmund Harkins vanished. Perhaps he would not ask of suspects. Of course he did.

I arrived at the castle amid much hustle and bustle. A lady's wagon was drawn up near the gatehouse, and a hempen canvas, bleached white, was being fitted over hoops so as to protect the inhabitants from the sun – which at that moment was obscured behind clouds. I recognized the wagon. It had brought Lady Emma and Rohilda to Bampton and was now apparently about to take them away.

Runcies were brought from the marshalsea and hitched to the wagon, and three palfreys also appeared, bridled and saddled for a journey. The door to the solar opened and Lord Gilbert emerged, then Sir Roger, Lady Emma, and Rohilda. The lass and her parents wore solemn expressions, although when Lord Gilbert spoke while descending the stairs to the castle yard Rohilda briefly smiled. Lord Gilbert, I decided, must intend to remain chaste. In which case he would continue to be chased.

Sir Roger's grooms appeared from the marshalsea. He and they mounted the palfreys, and Lady Emma and Rohilda were assisted into the wagon. Their aide was Sir Jaket Bec, and I thought he held Rohilda's hand longer than necessary as she ascended the step at the rear of the wagon. The lass smiled her thanks, and Sir Jaket bowed in return. Lord Gilbert may be immune to the lass's charms, but many men are not, and this includes Sir Jaket. And Richard, Lord Gilbert's son, from what I had seen a few days past. I wondered where the lad was this day.

Wishes for safe travel followed, with much waving of hands. The horses and wagon rumbled across the drawbridge and no more was seen of the comely Rohilda. Lord Gilbert turned away as the wagon crossed the forecourt, but Sir Jaket watched where the wagon had disappeared for some time. Perhaps Sir Roger had not snared the game he preferred, but he might be content with a buck could he not trap a stag.

"You have no thought as to who the men were the holy man saw in the Weald the night Edmund vanished?" Lord Gilbert said when in the solar I told him of what had transpired since we last spoke.

"None. Residents of the Weald, most likely. At least some of them were. Mayhap there was a man or two of Bampton."

"Aye, mayhap," my employer agreed. "I don't like to lose a tenant, even a rogue like Edmund, but even worse would be to lose the tenants who did away with him."

"If they were your tenants, and not the bishop's."

79

"Aye. If. Well, you did right to keep me informed, even if you had little to tell."

I departed the castle with my spirits as low as the clouds over the forest to the west. More rain threatened. I looked forward to the possibility. If the heavens opened I would have an excuse to retreat to Galen House and perch by my fire.

John Kellet appeared as I crossed Shill Brook. We met at Church View Street and I greeted the cadaverous priest.

"Sir Hugh," he replied. "You are well met. I was on my way to Galen House."

"Are you ill?" I asked.

"Nay. I do not seek your services. I wish to speak to you of a matter which presently troubles the town."

"Then come. We will enjoy cups of ale and you may tell me of the matter of which you speak."

I ushered Kellet into my hall, called for Adela to bring two cups of ale, then invited the priest to unburden himself. He looked to the open door and I divined his meaning. What he had to say was for my ears only. The open door meant that Adela would hear from the kitchen what he had to say. I closed it.

"A matter which troubles the town," I repeated. "Is it the slaying of Edmund Harkins of which you wish to speak?"

"Aye," he said softly. Evidently he did not trust a closed door to keep our conversation private. "I have recently heard a confession," he began.

"You are not permitted to speak of it," I said.

"I will not. The burden of knowledge is, however, heavy and I struggle with knowing things I cannot repeat."

I was puzzled. "Then why are you here? Why have you sought me?"

"I have asked myself whether or not I should for three days."

"And your answer?"

"I cannot tell of the confession I heard, but I can tell you what I did not hear."

"And what you did not hear might lead me to solving the mystery of Edmund Harkins' murder?"

"If you have the wit. But I warn you now that if you discover those who slew Edmund you may wish you had not."

"Those? More than one did the murder?"

The priest was silent. I already knew from the holy man's report that multiple men were likely involved in Harkins' death. And now it appeared that if I learned their names and made widows of their wives I might as well leave Bampton and my position serving Lord Gilbert. I would be forever despised.

"You provide a hint to send me after murderers, yet you wish I might fail? Is that your meaning?"

"I told you I struggle with this matter."

"What is your advice? Apparently from some man's confession you know who did the murder of Edmund Harkins, yet you warn me of dire consequences if I succeed in discovering the felons."

"I should not have come to you," Kellet said – softly. "No good will come of this. Evil was done, and more evil will result. It is evil that some may slay another and escape punishment for the deed. It would also be evil if they were found out and sent to a scaffold."

"Does it help you carry the burden now you have shared it with another?"

"Nay. I hoped it might."

The priest stood. "If you learn more and can tell me of it, do so," I said.

"You intend to persist in the search?"

"Aye. Even though it may be as you suggest, that no good will come from either success or failure."

I bade Kellet good day, and accompanied him to the door. I was puzzled by this strange encounter. Clouds yet hung low over the town, but no rain muddied the streets. I had no good excuse for remaining indoors by the fire.

There was at least one Bampton resident who knew what I did not. How to find that man and persuade him to speak? He was not likely to talk of deeds which would lead him to perform the sheriff's dance. But was that the confession which caused John Kellet to seek me? Mayhap he had heard some man admit that he knew who slew Edmund, but had not himself participated in the felony, and wished absolution not for what he did but for what he knew and would not tell.

Chapter 6

Next morning, after breaking my fast, I sought Walter and Osbert, Edmund's mates in the plow team. Autumn plowing was done for the season and men were busy at other labors, preparing for winter. Soon Martinmas would come and 'twould be time to slaughter animals which could not be fed through the winter and whose flesh would sustain folk through another dark, cold season. I reminded myself to seek Thomas Neckham and learn whose swine he had taken to the forest for pannaging.

Walter's wife told me he was at work in a wheat field to the east of the new tithe barn. I found him swinging a scythe, cutting the stalks of harvested grain down to the ground. The severed stems would be chopped fine and mixed with hay for winter fodder.

Walter saw me approach and rested upon the scythe. Clouds of the previous day had thinned and weak sunlight brightened the day, but did little to warm the morning. Nevertheless Walter perspired, his kirtle damp with sweat. There are few occupations which will warm a man so thoroughly as swinging a scythe.

Walter was silent as he watched me cross the strip he was cutting. I greeted the fellow with a smile and in return received a muttered reply from a visage carved in flint. He did manage to tug a forelock.

I had not spoken to Walter, or Osbert, since Edmund was found dead. The last conversation I had with the man was when Edmund had gone missing but was not yet found. Most, including Walter, I believe, thought at the time that he had run off. Walter and Osbert were angry that he had shirked his responsibility. His expression this morning led me to believe that my appearance reminded him of the event and caused his ire to reappear. He was angry, true enough, but not for the reason I suspected.

All Bampton residents suspected that if I appeared 'twas likely I would have questions about Edmund Harkins' slaying. So Walter was prepared.

"I give you good day," I said.

To which greeting Walter again muttered an unintelligible reply. He glanced to the sky as if to confirm my assertion.

"Cast your mind back to the Monday I found you and Osbert plowing, when Edmund had gone missing. At the time you had no thought as to where he might have gone. Since then he has been discovered slain, and is now buried in St. Beornwald's churchyard. No doubt you have considered his death. Have you any opinions now which you did not have that Monday?"

"Opinions 'bout what?" he said gruffly.

"Edmund's death. At the time you thought, I believe, that he had fled Bampton. Now that you know differently do you remember anything he might have said or done which could point to some enemy he feared?"

"Nay. Edmund didn't fear no man."

"Did he speak of anything he planned to do in the near future? You and he and Osbert had plowed several strips in the days before he disappeared, had you not?"

"Two," Walter said.

"What conversations did you have with him as you worked?"

Walter shrugged. "Nothin' I remember. Spoke of the weather an' harvest an' such."

"Nothing else? Nothing more personal?"

"Edmund wasn't a man to speak of such things," Walter said.

"Did he never speak of his family?"

"Of Leuca, you mean?"

"And the children."

"Complained of 'er."

"How so?"

"'Bout every way a man could."

"She could do nothing properly?" I asked.

"Not to 'ear Edmund talk."

"And now he's dead."

Since Edmund's demise was common knowledge, Walter evidently thought no confirmation of his mortality necessary. He made no reply.

"Have you heard men speak of Edmund's murder?" I asked. "Folk may speak to friends of suspicions they would not voice to their bailiff."

"The rogue's gone an' good riddance, most do say."

"And you? Do you say the same?"

"I didn't slay 'im, if that's your notion."

"But you are not sorry he's dead?"

"Nay. Name a man of Bampton who is."

He had me there. Men will be pleased to assist a bailiff or sheriff or constable to learn who may have slain a man well liked, of good report. But not a man like Edmund Harkins.

"If you hear gossip about Edmund's death, come to me," I said.

Walter's expression did not lead me to believe he would do so.

"Where is Osbert today?"

"Ditchin' along the road to Cowley's Corner. You gonna ask 'im what you asked me?"

"Probably. Will I hear different replies?"

"Not likely."

I didn't.

Osbert atte Brook was working just beyond the path to the holy man's hut, a few hundred paces from Cowley's Corner. Ditching is one of the few exercises which may warm a man as much as swinging a scythe.

Ditching and such like labor was once the purview of villeins and part of the week work they owed. But Lord Gilbert and his forbears had over the past decades ended villeinage at Bampton Manor, preferring to collect rents from free tenants. Ditching, however, still needed to be done if fields were to be properly drained and roads not become a sea of mud following rain or during the spring thaw. So John Prudhomme hired men in the autumn with Lord Gilbert's coins to clear ditches and drains. They were paid for the task, not for the time it took to do it. Hence the scowls from Osbert's three companions when I called him from the work.

Conversation with Osbert was much like that with Walter. He'd not seen Edmund since the day before he disappeared. Bampton had lost little because of Edmund's death. Nay, he'd heard no rumors of who might have slain the lout. If he did, he'd seek me. Now, might he return to work?

"One more question," I said. "Did Edmund have friends in the Weald?" Friends would not likely have slain him, but Edmund's friends might also be Leuca's friends, and her friends might.

Osbert shrugged. "Never spoke of friends."

"In the Weald?"

"There, or anywhere else," Osbert said. "Don't think 'e 'ad many friends."

His work was warm, so when atte Brook turned to join his companions he shucked his cotehardie to labor only in kirtle and chauces.

I began to suspect Edmund Harkins had no friends at all. If members of a man's plow team are not his friends, who would be? A man's friends should be those who know him well. A man whose few "friends" are those who know little of him is surely a knave.

Who had traveled to St. Andrew's Chapel recently? I thought on this as I passed the castle on my way back to Galen House for my dinner.

Kate and Adela had prepared leach lombard, a meal I much enjoy. Of course, there are few meals I do not enjoy. As usual, Bessie managed to consume her share whilst dominating the conversation and John simply forged ahead, wiping his trencher clean and looking about for any residue.

Adela, as had become her custom of late, ate silently and seemingly with little enjoyment. Something troubled the lass, but discerning the thoughts of a maid is beyond my ken. Mayhap Kate knew the cause of her melancholy. I resolved to speak to her of it that night.

Robert Baker's house lies at the eastern fringe of the village, near to Bushy Row. A place where sparks from his bake oven are not so likely to alight on someone's thatch and burn a house to cinders. Mayhap, I thought, Robert had seen a man not of John Kellet's tiny parish walking past his house toward St. Andrew's Chapel.

Robert's oven was cooling, his baking for the day done, when I rapped upon his door. He was just finishing his dinner, belched, greeted me, and asked how he might serve me.

The oven was attached to the front of his house, and due to its heat windows on either side were customarily open when the oven was lit. There was a reasonable chance that Robert would see folk who passed by on the High Street. Perhaps so many passed his door he would not take thought as to who had done so. The High Street is the main road east to Cote and eventually Oxford. Only a few would travel that way with St. Andrew's Chapel as their goal, and if they did would need to pass up Bushey Row to reach the chapel.

Among those who passed Robert Baker's house how many would turn from the High Street to seek John Kellet? Few. That I sought the baker is a measure of my frustration. The chance that he could identify a man walking to St. Andrew's Chapel was small. But what other acts of mine had led to the felon I sought?

"Four days past did you see a man of Bampton parish pass on his way to Bushey Row and thence to St. Andrew's Chapel?" I asked.

"Hmm. Four days, you say? Sunday, that would be?"

"Aye." I had not considered the days, just counted back from what John Kellet had said. Robert's oven would have been cold on Sunday, his skin windows closed. No man can be identified if seen through the oiled skin of a window. This visit, I decided, would be fruitless. Not so.

"Followed a fellow from St. Beornwald's Church after mass. 'E turned up Bushey Row."

"Who was it?"

"Don't know. Followin' behind, wasn't I."

"What did he wear?"

The baker scratched his head, shifting his cap askew, as if the exercise would help recall the event. "Brown cotehardie. Chauces was brown, too. Cap was gray, or maybe just dirty."

This description might have been of little help. Half the commons of England wear cotehardies of some shade of brown. Only the prosperous go to the expense of woad or madder to enliven the color of their apparel. However, common as such garb was, I remembered recently seeing a man so clothed. Osbert atte Brook wore brown chauces, had discarded a darker brown cotehardie when he returned to ditching, and wore a sweat-stained gray cap.

I thanked Robert for his time and set out for St. Andrew's Chapel. The structure is tiny, barely seven paces wide by twelve long, with a squat tower at the south end. Kellet lives in the tower in a chamber perhaps four paces square. The bell rope passes through this room, so the priest could ring the Angelus without leaving his bed, was he minded to do so. There is no porch, only a small roof extending an arm's length from the chapel wall above the door. Which is likely why the bottom of the door is rotting from the damp to which it is constantly exposed.

Hinges squealed when I pushed the door open, announcing to Kellet that he had a visitor. He appeared at the top of the stairs which led to his chamber. This stairway is so steep it might qualify as a ladder.

"Ah. . . Sir Hugh," he said, and carefully placed feet and hands upon the treads to lower himself to my level. "How may I serve you?"

"'Twas Osbert atte Brook who came to see you last Sunday for confession, was it not?" I said. I could not be certain of this with what small evidence I possessed, but thought the assertion might stir a telling reaction from the priest. It did.

Kellet's eyes widened and he lurched as if swatted across the skull with a barrel stave. His mouth opened to speak, and he swallowed like a pike tossed upon a riverbank. But no words followed, and within a few heartbeats he regained his composure.

"You know I cannot speak of what I hear in the confessional box."

"I do not ask you to do so. All I ask is corroboration of what I have learned in another way."

Kellet remained silent.

"You will not tell me if the confession you heard which so troubled you was that of Osbert atte Brook? I suspect if 'twas not you would be quick to say so. No denial – for that would be a lie and a sin – means, I think, that 'twas Osbert."

"Think what you wish. I will not say what I was told in the confessional and I will not say who said it."

"You must act as your conscience and the church requires. So must I. My conscience will not permit me to forsake the quest for a felon, and the Lord Christ demands His followers seek justice."

"There are those who would say justice has already been done," Kellet said.

"With the slaying of Edmund Harkins? Aye, I suppose so."

I left Father John standing at the foot of his vertical stairs and departed the chapel. I still did not know who had slain Edmund Harkins, but I felt sure I now knew of a man who did have that knowledge. And who had perhaps participated in dispatching him.

Kate and Adela prepared a simple supper of canabeans with bacon. Kate seemed to be regaining her appetite whilst Adela was losing hers, for the lass only toyed with her meal.

Days grow short, so 'twas near to dark when Adela departed Galen House for the Weald. I saw her glance to the north, toward the church, before she gathered her cloak about her and scurried off to the south and home.

When Bessie's ears were safely tucked abed, I asked Kate of Adela's melancholy. She knew the cause, but had feared telling me.

"She is sometimes followed to her home."

"Has some rogue accosted her? Threatened her?"

"In a manner, I suppose it might be said."

"Why did you fear telling me? I will visit the man and see that his behavior is modified."

"You would find it difficult. The man is not under your authority."

I was puzzled. What man of Bampton could ignore my commands?

"The fellow is of the Weald?" I said. "I will speak to Father Thomas. He will put a stop to the harassment."

"The man is not of the Weald. Father Thomas might speak to the fellow, but he will likely ignore him."

"You speak in riddles," I complained.

"I fear you will be precipitate when you know who threatens Adela. He is already a menace to you and if you make demands of him he will likely seek you harm."

"Father Harold? The new priest is troubling Adela?"

"Aye. But you must promise me you will not go to him. Or to Father Thomas. If you complain to Father Thomas, Father Harold will know. He will go to his uncle with accusations."

"What has he done to so frighten Adela?"

"He demands that she become his housekeeper. She told him that she is already employed but he will not listen."

"Housekeeper?"

"Aye. We know what that means. He intends to make her his mistress. He told her that if she will not relent, he will see to it that her father's rents are increased."

"The man is a poor cotter, barely able to keep the wolf from the door as it is," I said.

"Aye. This is why Adela may yield to him."

"She said this?"

"Yesterday."

"Tell her to put him off for a few weeks."

"What do you intend? Do not anger the priest, I pray you."

"Oh, he will be angry. No doubt of that. But his wrath will not cause me or any other harm."

"How can you avoid it? His uncle –"

"There is a man who outranks Bishop Brantyngham and who will be displeased to learn of Adela's trouble."

"Lord Gilbert?" Kate said. "But those of the Weald are not his tenants."

"True. But if I know Lord Gilbert, he will not countenance wickedness from a priest of his manor church."

I had intended to seek Osbert atte Brook after breaking my fast Friday, but decided Adela's plight was more pressing than Edmund Harkins'. He was dead and could be troubled no more. Adela lived and might be vexed continually by an amorous priest.

I waited to visit the castle until the sun was well up. And after several days of cloud and mist and fog, this day the sun was visible. I took this as a good omen.

Kate knew my destination when I departed Galen House but forbore mentioning it. Adela had arrived. At the door I whispered to Kate that she must persuade Adela to put off the scurrilous priest. "Tell her that I will accompany her to her home each night."

"If you do," Kate whispered in reply, "Father Harold will know she has told you of his misbehavior."

My Kate has a quick wit. I was forced to agree. But some way must be found to protect the lass from Father Harold's predation. I told Kate we must think on this. She agreed.

My employer does not rise early from his bed, especially as winter approaches and the sun appears later each morning. Which is why I did not plan to cross the drawbridge until the third hour, when I thought I would find Lord Gilbert between leaving his bed and preparing for dinner. My timing was excellent.

Lord Gilbert was warming himself before a fire in the solar. His son, Richard, accompanied him. The lad was once slender as a reed, all knees and elbows, but in the past year had begun to fill out and his resemblance to his father was striking.

"Have you come to tell me you have discovered who murdered Edmund?" Lord Gilbert began.

"Nay, although I believe within a few more days I may be able to do so. 'Tis another matter which needs your attention."

"My attention? You cannot deal with it?"

"Nay. 'Tis beyond a bailiff's license."

"You have my writ to do what is required to keep good order in Bampton. What issue can be beyond that?"

"Kate's maid, Adela, is beset by a man whose attention she does not seek."

"The lass is of the Weald, is she not? Tell one of the priests of St. Beornwald's to deal with it. Or is the fellow troubling her a tenant of mine?"

"Nay, the man is not of your manor, and Father Thomas and Father Ralph will be unable to help. 'Tis the new priest who is vexing the lass."

"How so?" Lord Gilbert scowled.

"He demands that she become his housekeeper. If she refuses he will raise her father's rents."

"Hmm. The lout must not be allowed to deal so with the lass. What do you suggest?"

"Send a letter to Bishop Brantyngham, closed with your seal, requesting... nay, demanding that Father Harold be reassigned."

"Should the bishop be told why?"

"Aye. Many priests have female housekeepers and Holy Church and their parish look the other way. But these women take the role willingly. They are not coerced."

"Indeed. I will call for my chaplain. Dictate such a message to him. I'll sign and seal it and send it tomorrow."

Richard had sat in a corner, listening to our exchange. Now he spoke. "I'll take the letter to the bishop," he volunteered.

"What? Alone on the road between here and Exeter? Nay, 'tis one hundred miles or more. . . closer to one hundred and fifty. I'll send Sir Jaket and his squire."

"Three men together will be safer than two if miscreants should descend upon them," Richard replied.

"You wish to accompany them? Very well. You should meet Bishop Brantyngham. You may have dealings with him at some future time."

Lord Gilbert sent John Chamberlain to fetch his chaplain. The priest serves also as Lord Gilbert's scrivener.

Like most nobles, my employer's education involved martial matters, not literacy. He can read and write, of course, in both English and French, but not well, so as with other concerns hires men to do for him what he cannot, or will not.

I spent the next hour with the chaplain, creating, I hoped, a message which would combine entreaty with demand. We finished just before dinner. Lord Gilbert read the missive, approved, and when I had folded it thrice applied his crest to the melted wax seal.

I wondered if Sir Jaket would appreciate being chosen for this mission. I learned later from John Chamberlain that he was, in fact, eager to make the journey. Sir Roger Wren's small manor is just south of Bath, three or so days' journey along the road to Exeter. Mayhap Richard also knew this and that is why he was enthusiastic to meet the Bishop of Exeter.

Chapter 7

Sir Jaket, Squire Thomas, and Richard would depart early Saturday morning for Exeter, Lord Gilbert's letter safely reposing in Sir Jaket's saddle bag. A reply could not be expected for ten days or so. Longer, if the fair Rohilda persuaded the travelers to interrupt their journey near Bath.

In the meantime I had to devise some way to keep Adela safe from Father Harold and pry from Osbert atte Brook what he had confessed to the priest of St. Andrew's Chapel. Atte Brook would probably be found near to Cowley's Corner, his work ditching not yet completed. Before I sought him I would return to Galen House and seek my dinner.

Kate and Adela had prepared eels in bruit and a compost, so even though 'twas a fast day I left the table well sated and prepared to look with a benevolent eye on all mankind.

Except for Father Harold. Whilst walking from castle to home a way to protect Adela had occurred to me. I whispered the solution to my Kate after dinner, while Adela was upstairs putting John to his crib for a nap. She agreed that the plan was feasible. If Father Thomas would agree.

I put aside seeking Osbert and went to Father Thomas's vicarage. I found him just rising from his dinner. 'Twas a mean pottage of some mixture. I nearly felt guilty for my savory repast. Nearly.

"Good day, Sir Hugh. How may I serve you?"

"'Tis not me who needs your service," I replied. "Are you assigned the noon Angelus today?"

"Aye. So happens I am. I was about to send my clerk to ring the bell."

"Good. I will accompany you to the church. There is a matter I must discuss with you, and privily. The church porch might serve."

The priest studied me, perplexed at my request, but agreed to meet me there. I set off for the church whilst Father Thomas donned his surplice. He arrived at the church but a few minutes after me.

"Now," he said. "What business have you for me which requires secrecy?"

"Kate's servant, Adela Parkin, needs your assistance."

"Indeed? How may a priest help a lass?"

"She is harassed by a man who demands she become his housekeeper, and we both know what that means."

"Why do you not deal with the fellow?"

"The man is your comrade Father Harold. If I confront him he will certainly deny the charge, and then send word to his uncle that I own heretical views. Much distress will follow."

"What do you want from me?" the priest said. "To speak to him? He will not regard any reproach from me. He has a powerful uncle."

"I had thought to escort Adela to her home each night, but Kate fears Father Harold will then assume Adela has told me of his imposition and he will go to his uncle with accusations."

"Hmm. So he might. But I still do not see what you want of me."

"Tell your clerk to come to Galen House every day at the ninth hour, whence he is to accompany Adela to the

Weald. If Father Harold sees this he will likely assume the lass has complained to you. What can he do to threaten you?"

The priest pursed his lips. "Not much," he finally said. "But for how long must this escort continue, and what should I tell Christopher?"

"Your new clerk knows little of folk in Bampton and the Weald. Tell him only that the maid is vexed by a man who follows her seeking her favors. Do not tell him 'tis Father Harold. Tomorrow Lord Gilbert will send a letter to Bishop Brantyngham demanding that Father Harold be assigned elsewhere."

"Lord Gilbert?"

"Indeed. Even the archbishop would take heed of Lord Gilbert Talbot's wishes."

"I will not be sorry to be rid of Father Harold. You believe the bishop will yield to Lord Gilbert?"

"Bishops are competent politicians. He will know that if he opposes Lord Gilbert he will be outmatched. And he will consider what is to be gained if he refuses to replace his nephew compared to gaining Lord Gilbert's favor if he does."

"Hah. You might be a politician yourself," Father Thomas chuckled. "Very well. I will do as you ask. Christopher will be at Galen House at the ninth hour. He will not resent being assigned to walk with a pert maid, I think. But if he's seen doing so each day gossip will follow."

"True. Perhaps you could tell Father Ralph of this matter, and his clerk could replace Christopher every third or fourth day."

"A fair suggestion. Father Ralph was at first pleased with Father Harold, but the bloom has faded from that rose."

As I turned to leave the church porch the clerk arrived to ring the Angelus bell. When he had entered the church Father Thomas asked of my investigation into Edmund Harkins' death.

"I have a clue," I replied.

"But you cannot yet put a name to the guilty man?"

"Nay."

I thought Father Thomas appeared relieved as he turned to follow his clerk. His opinion, I knew, was much the same as John Kellet's; little good could come from hanging a man who had rid the town of a villain.

A half-dozen or so of Bampton's elderly residents approached the church as I passed through the lychgate. These were folk whose aching bones reminded them daily that they would soon meet St. Peter at the gates of pearl. They did not wish to be negligent in worship as the critical day and hour drew near, so when the Angelus bell sounded they tottered to the church, hoping to accumulate treasure in heaven to make up for the treasures on earth most had failed to gather.

Osbert atte Brook and his companions were, as I had thought, yet at work with shovel and mattock hollowing out the ditches on the road to Cowley's Corner before winter snow and rain could fill them with water.

The man saw me approach when I had barely passed the castle and I thought even at a distance I could see him sigh with exasperation. What else may cause a man to sigh? Fear? Nay. A man may quake in fear, but not sigh. Osbert's expression told me he considered me an annoyance, not a threat. I was about to modify his view.

I was an annoyance to Osbert's companions also. When I took him from the work, I added to their labor. Bailiffs become accustomed to the animus of those they govern. In my case this dislike is tempered due to my profession. If I have stitched a lad's wound – and small boys are partial to conduct which leads to bruises, lacerations, and broken bones – his father is in future likely to view me charitably.

I called to Osbert to set aside his spade and join me at the side of the road. Another sigh and roll of the eyes, but he did so. I then commanded that he follow me. I took him to the path leading to the holy man's hut, thence beyond to the place where hogs had unearthed Edmund Harkins' corpse. No man had yet refilled the hole.

We stood in silence, gazing into the shallow depression. I have learned that sometimes the best answers come after unasked questions. A guilty man's conscience, if he has one, may trouble him so that he might blurt out words to fill an awkward silence. This tactic is not always successful. A man may practice a vice so long that he comes to believe it a virtue.

So I waited for Osbert to comment upon what he saw. Finally, he did. "This where them pigs found Edmund?" he said.

"Indeed. You have not before visited the place?"

"Nay. Was told 'twas near to the holy man's hut."

"The hogs did awful carnage to Edmund," I said. "Devoured his entrails down to the backbone. Ribs all askew. Hadn't consumed his face yet, so he could be identified. A terrible thing. . . that men would so abuse another as to put him in such a place, dead, in unhallowed ground."

"Aye," Osbert muttered softly.

"And you know who did this villainy."

"Nay," he said with vehemence. No quiet murmuring this time. "Who says so? The scoundrel lies."

"You were seen a few days past entering St. Andrew's Chapel. You are not of that parish. Why would you go there if not to confess to the priest that you had sinned? And what great evil has visited Bampton? The murder of Edmund Harkins."

"Did that priest say I'd confessed to slaying Edmund? If so, he lies."

"Father John would not betray the confessional. I have put circumstances and events in order and they seem to point to your complicity in Edmund's death."

Here was a leap into the unknown. But occasionally bailiffs learn useful things by pretending to know more than they do.

"I didn't slay 'im an' I don't know who did."

"Your confession to John Kellet was of another matter?"

"Aye, an' I'll tell you of it, do you promise to tell no other."

Here was a startling offer. Did I need, or want, to know of other evils in my bailiwick? And it must be some evil which Osbert had confessed. Men do not seek absolution for good deeds they have done.

"I cannot make such a pledge," I replied. "I serve Lord Gilbert and one of my duties is to see that miscreants are punished for the wrongs they do. If men could do wickedness and escape the penalty due them, who then would obey the laws of God and men?"

"Then I must remain silent. You may think of me what you will. Father John has assigned me penance for the wrong I did."

"Have you performed this obligation?"

"Not yet, but I will do so. I do not wish to suffer in purgatory for such a trifle."

"A trifle, you say? Have you stolen some object? What penance did Kellet assign?"

Osbert did not immediately reply. He stared at his feet and the open grave a moment before he spoke.

"I am to return what I stole or pay tuppence to her I took it from. Then I must light candles and pay another tuppence to the chapel for prayers for my soul."

"Have you returned the stolen goods?"

"Not yet. Sold it. I must find the coin to buy it back. Or purchase another as good. So Father John requires."

"You took something from a woman? Is she of Bampton? No one has come to me complaining that a possession has vanished. You are fortunate that the theft has not been reported and you found out. You know Lord Gilbert has the right of infangenthef and Bampton has several likely oaks where a man might dangle for his wickedness."

"I hope to return what I pilfered before 'tis missed," Osbert said softly.

"So if I go to John Kellet and speak to him of this tale he will corroborate what you have said?"

"Suppose so, if he don't think to do so would be breakin' 'is vows."

There was yet an hour before darkness would envelope the town. I sent Osbert back to his companions and hastened from one end of Bampton to the other. I wished to confront Father John with Osbert's confession whilst his words were yet fresh in my mind.

"This is most peculiar," Kellet said when I told him of Osbert's confession. "I am constrained from speaking of what I was told, but Osbert, I suppose, is under no such restraint."

"You believe what he confessed? That he stole an object?"

"Why would a man confess to a theft he did not do?"

"Indeed. Then again, why would a man take something of such small worth and thereby imperil his soul? Eternity in hell for tuppence?"

Kellet shrugged. "Because the opportunity arose."

"What is it he stole? Would telling me break the seal of confession?"

"I suppose, as Osbert has told you so much, there is no harm in completing the account. 'Twas a spoon. A pewter spoon."

"How would a man gain access to another's spoons?"

"When a house is empty another may enter without challenge. 'Twas when folk were at church, to bury Edmund Harkins."

"I was present. There were few mourners."

"Aye, few. Leuca and her children and a few others."

"Osbert entered Leuca's house whilst she was at her husband's funeral?" I said.

"He admitted so. Took the spoon from the bottom of a small chest."

Here was why Leuca had not reported the theft. Most folk use wooden spoons. Leuca probably kept her pewter spoon for some special use, if any special occasion occurred in her cheerless life.

"I told Osbert," I said, "that he is fortunate to be above the sod. If he had been taken with the spoon in his possession Lord Gilbert could have invoked infangenthef."

"Indeed. Did he also tell you what I require for absolution?"

"Aye. 'Tis a small punishment for theft, but laborers are few since pestilence has come and come again. If Lord Gilbert should ever hear of your leniency he will forgive.

He surely does not want to lose another tenant, this one to a noose."

'Twas nearly dark when I turned to Church View Street and home. Ahead of me, near to the church, I saw the shadow of a man walking briskly. His back was to me, and he wore either a robe or a long, dark cotehardie. Most men young enough to walk so energetically wear cotehardies short enough to show a manly leg. I do. So likely it was a robe the walker wore. Father Harold? Returning to his vicarage? Was he returning after following Adela to the Weald?

I entered Galen House, barred the door behind me against the night, and sought Kate and my supper. She was busy cleaning pease pottage from John's cheeks but took time from the task to greet me with a kiss. Bessie has learned to dine with less ardor, and looked on with some distaste as her mother dealt with her brother's unsophisticated gustatory conduct.

"Did Adela depart for home in good time?" I asked Kate.

"Aye. She's been away since the ninth hour."

"Good. I saw what I believed to be a priest or a clerk walking near to St. Beornwald's just now and feared it might have been Father Harold returning after accosting her."

"Nay. She's been away for some time."

"Tomorrow, and for a week or two after, either the clerk to Father Thomas or the clerk to Father Ralph will call at the ninth hour and accompany Adela to the Weald. I hope after Sir Jaket returns from Exeter such precaution will no longer be necessary."

"This will cheer Adela. I told her that she must have faith that you will help her escape Father Harold's badgering and she must not give in to him."

"Did she believe you?"

"I think so. But her countenance is quite fallen. Perhaps the burden oppressing her is greater than a threat from an offensive priest."

When the day began I'd had hopes that, when it ended, I would be near to assigning guilt to those who slew Edmund Harkins. But I was no closer to doing so now than at dawn. Farther, even, from the solution to the wickedness, for as I sat to my supper what I had assumed in the morning I now knew to be false.

I broke my fast Saturday morning with a maslin loaf. 'Twas our last loaf, so Kate gave Adela coins and sent her to Robert Baker for fresh loaves. Again, as she departed, I saw Adela hesitate at the door and peer in both directions. When she was assured the street offered no hazard she darted away.

I had plans for the morning, but waited for Adela's return before setting off. I called first at the castle and learned that Sir Jaket, Thomas, and Richard had departed for Exeter at first light. Charles de Burgh, Lord Gilbert's nephew, the son of his widowed sister, had begged, John Chamberlain said, to accompany the travelers, but Lord Gilbert was adamant that he remain. The lad was a year older than Bessie and had been given to Lord Gilbert's care for instruction in chivalry and the manly arts. But these he had not yet mastered and Lord Gilbert would not permit him to leave the safety of Bampton Castle.

The lad's mother, Lady Joan Talbot de Burgh, resides near Banbury. Before I met my Kate, whilst I was yet a bachelor, I had esteemed Lady Joan from afar, and she, I believe, thought highly of me. But the difference in our stations forbade more than mutual admiration. Then, on a visit to Oxford, I met Kate, and my life has been much enriched.

I once heard a wandering friar preach to a scattering of folk in Oxford. He decried the disparity between rich and poor, and asked if the Lord Christ created the world for the benefit of gentlemen and their ladies. "The only difference I see between folk," he concluded, "is that some he created women, and for this, much thanks."

I agree.

I strolled from the castle through Bampton's streets and lanes, inspecting my bailiwick and hoping my eyes might fall upon some thing or man which would stir my thoughts toward discovering a murderer. Folk were busy at the affairs of autumn. Lord Gilbert's tenants have the right to collect fallen branches in the forest and I saw several families – husbands, wives, and all but the smallest children – with armloads of oak and beech limbs. The collection would help to warm them and their pottage in the months to come.

Usually when I am out upon Bampton's streets the men I meet greet me pleasantly and tug a forelock, desirous of good standing with their lord's official. But this day those I met seemed to avoid my gaze, as if something in an adjoining meadow had caught their attention. I arrived at Galen House for my dinner having exchanged conversation with no man since leaving the castle. My duty to seek a murderer, I thought, was not popular.

Kate and Adela had prepared blancmange for our dinner. As we ate I mentioned to Kate the chilly reception my travel through the town had received. Kate's reply surprised me, although perhaps it should not have.

"'Tis the same with me. When I leave Galen House on some task the women I meet seem to go out of their way to ignore me. This never used to be. Women of Bampton wanted to be on good terms with their bailiff's wife."

"But no longer?" I said.

"Aye. I've not had a conversation with another woman of Bampton for more than a week. If one passes on the street she might wish me good day, but will then hasten away before I can reply."

Adela had heard and watched this conversation, eyes flicking from me to Kate and back again. The lass ate sparingly. Now that Kate had found her appetite Adela seemed to have lost hers. And the cat had her tongue. A few weeks past she was as voluble as Bessie, but no longer. She finished her meal and began cleaning up the scraps. She knew her duties and went to work without being instructed. Perhaps, when Sir Jaket and his companions returned from Exeter they would bear news which would bring a sparkle back to the lass's eyes.

I told Adela that Father Thomas's clerk would call for her at the ninth hour, then I set out to join John Prudhomme. Together we had planned to observe whilst villeins and a few of Lord Gilbert's tenants and grooms spread marl and manure upon his demesne lands. Next week sheep would be loosed into these strips so their droppings would also enrich the soil before spring plowing.

Uctred was one of the grooms at work spreading straw and manure from Lord Gilbert's marshalsea. He and his friend Arthur had assisted me many times when extra muscle was required to subdue a miscreant, although Uctred was at least three stone lighter than Arthur Wagge had been. Those spreading manure and marl took my appearance as an excuse to lean upon their rakes for respite from the labor. Uctred glanced to me and tugged a forelock. A tenant dumping manure from a handcart nearby saw Uctred's silent greeting and frowned. I exchanged a few words with Uctred, then went on my way.

The matter of Edmund Harkins' murder was driving me to a solitary life. And Kate also. Villagers of Bampton were making it clear they objected to my search for Edmund's slayer. What more might they do if I was successful? I wondered if I wanted to be.

Where would Kate and I go if the folk of Bampton would have nothing to do with us? Would my service to Lord Gilbert as his bailiff become impossible? I suppose some would yet seek my services as surgeon if they had been incautious with a mattock and injured a foot, or if a son fell from one of Lord Gilbert's apple trees whilst filching fruit and required a broken arm be set.

I could make a living in Oxford. The town is filled with physicians diagnosing ills by sniffing men's urine and prescribing foods to alter a man's bile. Most of these will not deign to stitch a wound and would not even know how to. But Kate resided in Oxford for several years and she does not speak as if she would like to return, nor does she remark how pleasant it was to live amid the stink of Oxford's filthy streets

John and I left the grooms, tenants, and villeins to their work and traveled to our respective homes. As I turned to Church View Street I saw Adela and Christopher appear. They did not at first notice me, a hundred paces away, so engrossed were they in conversation.

A clerk has not yet taken holy orders. I suspect that even doing so would not make a lad immune to the charms of a pert lass. And the clerk was a handsome lad, tall and with a strong chin just beginning to show whiskers. No wonder Adela seemed pleased with his company. What had I done?

Adela and the clerk spoke a greeting when they passed. Briefly. Then returned to their conversation. Whatever business had made Adela melancholic was no longer in evidence. She smiled, which I had not seen her do for two weeks.

The willow bark and monk's hood I had collected two weeks past had been drying in Galen House kitchen. 'Twas time to crush the physics to a fine powder and fill some vials with the stuff. The vial with monk's hood I would deposit in my small chest, which is equipped with a lock. Bessie is an inquisitive child. I would not have her find the vial and taste the discovery.

As I crushed the monk's-hood root my mind wandered back to the day I had pulled the plants from the ground. Willows grew thickly along the bank of Shill Brook, but monk's hood prefers a well-drained soil. I had found the herb twenty or so paces from the stream up a gentle slope. I knew where I would find it, for I had uprooted such plants there in years past.

I had not been the only person to seek monk's hood there. It occurred to me now, as I worked mortar and pestle, that I had seen a place where fresh soil indicated some plant had been uprooted. Monk's hood? Or some other verdure? What vegetation grew there which some man would draw from the ground? For that matter, if someone did pull up a monk's-hood root, why would he do so? To make an oil to soothe his aching joints? Or for some other more malign purpose?

I finished pounding the monk's-hood root to granules, then filled a vial with the flakes and stopped the container with a wooden plug. This I then placed in the small, secure chest. Only when the monk's hood was safely put away did I seek Kate to tell her I was off, but would return well before dark for my supper. So I intended.

Chapter 8

What I might learn from visiting the place where I had plucked three monk's-hood plants from the earth I could not say. Crouching in the back of my mind was the thought that Edmund Harkins' death had something to do with poison, although I'd tried to dismiss the thought. Had I not seen Leuca drink from the same ewer and eat from the same pot as Edmund? And was the woman not genuinely dismayed when her husband disappeared? If not, she was a cunning player.

Yet someone and something had slain Edmund. If 'twas not poison, then a dagger in the belly, mayhap? After the hogs had feasted upon his gut no wound made by a blade would be found. Could those who buried him know this? That scavenging pigs would obscure a gash in the belly? Not likely.

I walked the path through the Weald as men were returning to their homes from the day's labor in the fields. As I expected, no man greeted me and most did their best to avoid meeting my eye. From the end of the lane I retraced my steps and came to the place where I had uprooted three monk's-hood plants. Many more plants were scattered about the area. The purple flowers had long since wilted, but I recognized the foliage. I saw loosened dirt where I had plucked three plants, and a few paces from the place I saw another small patch of soil where a fourth root had been drawn free of the earth.

'Twas as I remembered. Rain in the past days had blended the open holes with surrounding sod, but the openings were yet visible.

I know of no purpose for monk's hood but to relieve the ache of ageing knees and elbows, or to cause death. Carefully administered, a few grains of the powdered root may be consumed to dull pain. But, as I have written, I will not use it for that purpose. There are other, safer herbs. Too much monk's hood will end pain permanently and send a man to the churchyard.

I must hurry away or be late for my supper. Clouds had obscured the sun, so darkness came early this day. I turned from examining the tangle of weeds and grasses where grew the monk's hood and as I did heard something like the snapping of a twig. I turned toward the sound but saw nothing. Not surprising, as the verge of a small copse of oak and beech trees shadowed the place where I stood. I heard nothing more, so set off for the Weald and thence home. Before I reached Galen House I was required to make a detour.

My path to the end of the lane bisecting the Weald took me but a few paces from the now-dark copse. A moment later I heard not just the sound of a snapping twig but the din of an army stumbling through fallen leaves and branches.

I turned in the direction of this discord and saw men running, stumbling in the dark. 'Twas no army, even if in my startled state I thought it might be. Three men aimed their course toward me. I was too surprised to take cognizance of who so suddenly appeared, and when they closed to within a few paces I saw they had smeared their faces with some dark substance. Wet ashes, mayhap.

There could be but one reason for that. They did not wish to be recognized. This my addled brain deduced as being a danger to my well-being. I ran.

But not far.

Folk who roamed the forest collecting winter fuel had missed a small limb. I found it. My left ankle turned under me and I fell headlong. My pursuers were instantly upon me and I felt my arms and legs in the grip of men who can draw a bow of such power it can propel an arrow half a mile. There was no escaping their grasp.

My assailants said nothing. Evidently what they did next had been planned. Not much scheming was required. I was carried twenty paces of so toward Shill Brook and tossed in.

The brook in that location is little more than knee deep, so I was in no danger of drowning. And, unlike most men, I can swim. The skill came through being flung into the Wyre by my older brothers. That placid river flowed past my boyhood home, Little Singleton, and my brothers considered the activity great sport. Especially when no other engaging pastime presented itself.

I spluttered to my feet in the cold stream and heard one of the dark figures upon the bank finally speak: "Leave it be." Then, as quickly as they had appeared, my assailants vanished into the deepening gloom.

"Leave it be." These words had been carved into Galen House door. Surely the same man who did that had been one of those who pitched me into Shill Brook. He might have used his dagger to end my life, but did not. Not yet. But if I refused to "leave it be" might my life be in some danger? Such thoughts flashed through my mind as I scrambled and slipped from brook to bank and thence dry ground. I removed my cap, brushed hands through my hair, and tried to wring water from the hem of my cotehardie. Then, teeth chattering, I set off for home.

I studied each house I passed in the Weald to see if any man gazed from a dark window or peered around a corner to watch me pass. None did – that I could see.

Kate had not expected me to arrive home so late, nor had she expected that when I did I would drip water on the flags of her kitchen, my arms covered in gooseflesh.

I was cold and hungry. Both conditions could be rectified, but not before Kate heard what had befallen me. Bessie and John were abed, so I explained whilst I removed cotehardie and chauces and hung them before the fire. My braes and kirtle were yet soaked, but the linen would sooner dry than wool.

"They might have slain you," Kate said as she spooned up a dish of sops in fennel for my supper.

"They did not; nor do I believe they want to," I replied. "What they want is for me to ignore the murder of Edmund Harkins."

"Will you? Nay. I know my husband."

"Do you want me to allow those who slew Harkins to escape justice?"

"What is justice. . . in the matter of Edmund Harkins?" she asked.

"Does justice change depending upon the person wronged?"

"I don't know. Probably not. You should ask Dr. Wycliffe."

"He is not here. I must follow my own wit."

"Do not make a widow of me."

"If you become a widow 'twill be some other man's doing, not my own."

"You jest at my worry."

"Nay, wife. 'Tis but the truth. So far as I am able I intend to remain alive."

"It seems to me, after what has just happened to you, that you will find it easier if you allow Edmund to rest unavenged in his grave."

"The easiest course is often the wrong one. Indeed, the most worthy acts are frequently the most difficult."

"I thought I had wed a surgeon. Now I see I am wife to a philosopher," Kate said.

I finished the sops in fennel and with my back to the fire I was nearly dry. Dry enough to seek my bed. I lay awake well into the night, considering what had happened and what might have happened, and Kate's concern. How could I calm her fears yet continue to seek a felon? When I finally fell to sleep I had no answer.

Like most folk I do not break my fast Sunday mornings before mass. I contented myself with a cup of ale to assuage my thirst and growling stomach.

But for a seam, my chauces and cotehardie were now dry. I plucked a few strands of weed from the garments and donned them. They had shrunk. Or overnight I had gained a stone.

Kate noticed. "You will have to wear your old cotehardie 'til I can make you a new garment."

"The chauces will serve," I said. "No need to make new, and I have an old but serviceable pair in my chest."

"Will Shillside will have wool," Kate said. "What color would you like for a new cotehardie?

If he does not have your choice I can always have Adela dye what he may have."

"Green," I said. "'Tis a common enough hue. He is likely to have a bolt." Folk were beginning to pass Galen House on their way to St. Beornwald's Church. Kate had Bessie and John fed and ready, but I stopped her at the door. "Not yet," I said.

Kate peered at me, puzzled. "We will be late," she said.

"Not greatly. I want to watch as men pass Galen House to see if some look overlong at our home."

"You seek a guilty face?" she asked.

"Aye. Guilty men will pass here, this is sure. Whether or not they will display their guilt is another matter."

Kate and Adela entertained Bessie and John in the kitchen whilst I stood back from a front window and watched families pass by Galen House. The ground floor windows are of glass, so if any man glanced in my direction I could clearly see.

Nearly all who passed, both men and women, looked to Galen House. And in many faces I read distaste. Or was this my imagination? Did I see what I sought? I called for Kate and Adela as the last worshipers hurried past and the church bell rang. We followed these latecomers through the church porch.

Kate had glanced to me with questioning eyes as we hastened under the lychgate.

"I will tell you later," I said, and looked to Adela and Bessie. Kate nodded.

Father Harold rarely took his eyes from me during mass. So it seemed. Perhaps I had a guilty conscience for thwarting his scheme. Or mayhap he guessed who it was who frustrated his plot. Whatever the answer the priest gazed over his congregation with a black expression, seemingly lost in thought. Perhaps because it was unfamiliar territory. And when he passed the pax board his visage did not speak of peace and good will to men.

I was making enemies at a rapid pace. How many friends remained? Father Thomas? Aye, and probably Father Ralph. Lord Gilbert? Surely. For now. Uctred? Mayhap. The holy man? I believe so. Leuca Harkins? Questionable. Adela? Could a servant also be a friend when stations are so different? Probably not. Most bailiffs are accustomed to being friendless. Work collecting a lord's rents and fines sets men against them 'til their only friends are power and wealth. Even these are difficult to keep.

Dinner this day was capon farced. While it was roasting I sat at my table and put pen to parchment, writing more of the story of Edmund Harkins' death. As I wrote of what had passed I thought of what might come. Most of the possibilities seemed bleak. Speculation did nothing to improve my appetite.

When a knock sounded on Galen House door near to the ninth hour I thought 'twas Christopher, eager to walk with Adela to the Weald.

Not so. 'Twas Charles de Burgh. The lad was red-faced and out of breath. "Sir Hugh," he puffed, "my uncle desires that you attend him forthwith."

"Is he ill, or injured?"

"Nay. 'Tis a groom who needs your services."

"Injured?"

"Aye, stabbed."

"Tell Lord Gilbert I must assemble instruments and will hurry. Run, now. I'll be along directly."

I raced up the stairs to my chest, gathered scalpel, needles, and silken thread, then clattered down to the ground floor. Kate had heard the lad's summons and awaited me at the door.

"Who would risk Lord Gilbert's wrath by slaying a groom?" she asked.

"I'll soon know," I said, then kissed her and hurried to the castle.

John Chamberlain awaited me at the drawbridge. "This way," he said. "In the hall."

"Who is stabbed?"

"Uctred."

"Who did this?"

"No man knows."

"Uctred cannot say? Is he dead?"

"He lives, but near to death."

This conversation took place whilst I hurried with John to the hall. One of the trestle tables had been erected and I saw Uctred stretched upon it. Some man had tried to stop the bleeding from his wound. Unsuccessfully. His tunic had been stripped away and some linen garment bunched over the wound, under his kirtle. Gore dripped from the table to the flags below. Lord Gilbert, two valets, John Chamberlain, and the lad, Charles, stood helplessly gazing down on the motionless groom.

Uctred was white for loss of blood but for his lips. They were a ghastly blue. As I bent over him to take stock of his hurt I saw his chest rise and fall. Barely.

I dropped my instruments bag to the flags, called for more linen and a ewer of wine, then lifted Uctred's kirtle and pulled the soaked linen from the cut.

A dagger had entered his body between the lower ribs on his right side. When I removed the linen, blood flowed again, pulsing with each beat of Uctred's heart. If the dagger had not entered his heart – and I did not believe it had, else he would be dead – it had damaged some artery near to that organ. No surgeon I know of has written of the use of a man's heart to his body, but my observation, with Uctred and other bleeding wounds near the heart, persuades me that the heart is in some way connected to the flow of a man's blood.

I had no time to consider this notion. One of the valets ran up with a length of portpain from the pantry, and a few steps behind him came the other valet with a ewer of wine from the buttery.

I ripped off a section of the linen, used it to mop up Uctred's blood, then I dipped another linen swatch in the wine and swabbed the cut. A wound bathed in wine heals better than one not so cleansed, although no man knows why.

I would have liked to probe the cut for the damaged blood vessel and try to cauterize it, but no sooner did I stay the flow of blood and make the wound visible than another gush of blood obscured the cut. There was nothing else to do but stitch the cut closed and pray for the best. Which is what I did.

Speed was required, not neatness. I asked one of the valets to press a clean linen patch against the wound whilst I threaded a needle. This the fellow did, but not willingly. I saw his lip curl at the request. He dared not refuse. Lord Gilbert stood looking over his shoulder.

With my threaded needle I made six quick sutures and pulled them tight. The cut was a stab, not a slash, so few stitches were required. I was pleased to see that what had been a copious flow of blood was reduced to a slight seepage. And I knew from experience this would likely soon cease.

I took another linen fragment, soaked it in wine, and again bathed the wound. I thought I saw Uctred wince as the wine touched the cut. I took this for a good sign.

Lord Gilbert had peered over my shoulder as I closed the wound. "What is now to be done?" he asked. "Will you apply a salve before you bandage the wound?"

Each time I deal with such a laceration I am required to explain that I follow the practice of Henri de Mondeville, surgeon to the army of the King of France. De Mondeville discovered that wounds left open to the air, bathed only with wine, heal better than those smeared with salves and covered.

"If Uctred is to survive," I said, "he must have care for the next week or two."

"I will see to it," Lord Gilbert said. "Cicely Wagge will be willing, I think. Her Arthur and Uctred were close friends."

Willing or not, when your lord commands you to do a thing, you'd best do it.

"Get a pallet," Lord Gilbert said to one of the valets, "and take him to the great chamber under the solar. Carefully. Don't jolt him about. Geoffrey," he said to the valet, "remain with Uctred and when he regains his senses seek me. We must know who did this felony."

"If," I said.

"What?"

"If he regains his senses."

"You have doubts?"

"Important organs are close to the path the dagger followed when he was struck down: liver, spleen, even kidneys. He bled copiously, so I believe his spleen may have been pierced."

"Oh. Well. . . seek me if he dies, then."

"Where did the attack take place?" I asked. "Where was Uctred found? Who found him?"

"He was found near to the moat, opposite the gatehouse," John Chamberlain answered. "Nicholas Pervis was walking the parapet and saw him fall. Nearly toppled into the moat."

"I'd like to speak to Nicholas," I said.

"Bring him to the solar," Lord Gilbert instructed his chamberlain. "We will learn more of this felony there. By heavens, no man will strike down a retainer of mine and escape."

I didn't point out that the guilty man might also be a retainer.

Lord Gilbert and I took the inside stairs to the solar whilst three grooms appeared with buckets and mops to clean bloodstains from the floor of the hall. A Sunday supper would soon be served, and the gore would do no man's appetite good.

The fire in the solar had burned low. Lord Gilbert called for a groom to replenish the fuel, and as he did so John appeared with a lad barely past the age of a page. The youth glanced about apprehensively, taking in the colorful window glass, the embroidered wall hangings, and the cushioned chair which his lord occupied. He had certainly never before entered the chamber.

Lord Gilbert looked to me and nodded. I was to take the lead in this investigation. Well, that's what he pays me for.

"You were first to see Uctred, I am told. Is this so?"

The lad nodded.

"Speak up," Lord Gilbert said.

"Where were you, and where was he, when you saw him?"

"I were walkin' the parapet. I seen Uctred comin' toward the moat, staggerin', like. 'E was 'oldin' 'is side an' fell down. Got back up, but come near to fallin' in the moat. That's when I ran to get help."

I looked to John, then to Lord Gilbert. "Has Uctred enemies among your retainers?"

"None that I've heard of," my employer replied. He then looked to John.

The chamberlain shook his head. "If Uctred was disliked, I never heard of it. Nor, so far as I know, did he harbor ill feelings toward any other."

"When men arrived to help Uctred was he able to speak?"

"Nay," John replied. "Nicholas found me first, told what he'd seen, and I ran round the moat and found Uctred. He was senseless. No man has been able to get a word from him. I thought he was dead when I first found him."

"Does any man know where the attack took place?" I asked, looking to Nicholas.

"Nay," the lad answered. "When I seen 'im 'e was already pierced an' no other man near."

"Show me the place where he fell."

We left the solar, and Nicholas and John led me across the drawbridge and around the moat to the opposite side of the castle. The lad pointed to a place where men had stood and beaten down the grass. In the center of the beaten patch was a stain of drying blood.

Uctred had lost so much blood that I thought a trail of drops might lead to the place where he was struck down. 'Twas not easy to find and follow the blood trail. If I missed a drop Nicholas, with the keen eyes of youth, found it. The trail led to the Ladywell and there it ended in a stain which had soaked into the soil.

Lord Gilbert saw, and spoke. "Why had he come here?"

"He complained that he could not see well," John said. "His vision was clouded."

Folk often come to the Ladywell to pray and bathe their eyes with water if their sight is failing them. 'Tis believed that the spirit of St. Frideswide will intercede with the Lord Christ and restore a man's vision. Was Uctred kneeling, eyes closed in prayer, when he was struck down? This seemed possible.

The church teaches that only prayers spoken aloud are heard in heaven. If Uctred was beseeching the saint for aid, eyes closed, he might have neither seen nor heard his assailant approach. A man could step soundlessly in the soft grass which surrounded the well, and he could hide in wait in a small copse of crab apple trees which grew but five or six paces from the well. The foliage was nearly gone from the grove, but a man could successfully lose himself amongst the scrubby trees, especially if his prey was unwary.

I circled around the Ladywell, then walked to the crab apple grove, not knowing what I was seeking, but hoping some clue would offer itself. I found a dagger nearly hidden in the grass not three paces from the dried pool of blood. A slight reddish-brown stain on the blade told that it had recently been used. Was this the weapon used against Uctred? If so, why did his assailant abandon it? Or was this Uctred's dagger, used to defend himself, but dropped when he staggered toward the castle seeking aid?

I lifted the dagger from the grass for a closer inspection. 'Twas a mean weapon, made of iron rather than steel. The hilt was wrapped in well-worn leather, and the blade showed evidence of being broken and welded back to service. I had seen Uctred's dagger. This looked much like his.

Lord Gilbert saw me examining the dagger and asked to see it. One does not say no to a baron of the realm. I was not done examining the weapon, but handed it to him.

"Of poor quality," he observed, "and old. But sharp. Little rust except close to the edge."

"See the bloodstain?" I said. "'Tis not rust."

"Hah! Then this is the dagger used against Uctred. We find its owner and we will know the felon."

"This may be Uctred's dagger," I said.

Lord Gilbert scowled. "Then 'twill not help in discovering his assailant. Pity."

"It may," I replied.

"How so?"

"If 'tis Uctred's dagger, as I believe, he bloodied the edge against the man who tried to slay him."

"Ah. . . just so. You recognize it as Uctred's?"

"If not his 'tis very much like his. I recollect seeing his dagger."

"So we seek a man who has a new wound and he will be the rogue who pierced Uctred."

"Likely. But unlikely he will seek me to stitch up his cut."

"May depend upon how bad his wound is," John said, "and where the cut may be. If Uctred slashed his attacker's arm the fellow might not invent a good reason for such an injury. But I suppose if Uctred caught the man in the leg he might claim he'd struck his leg with a misaimed blow from axe or mattock."

"We must hope," I said, "that Uctred recovers from his wound. Not only because he is a good man and does not deserve to die in such a manner, but because if he regains his wits he may be able to tell who attacked him."

He did, but could not.

Chapter 9

*L*ord Gilbert keeps hounds for hunting. I suggested to him that he have his fewterer bring some of the dogs to the Ladywell. Perhaps they might discover and follow the scent of Uctred's assailant.

Lord Gilbert sent John to the castle and he returned shortly with the fewterer.

"Launcelot an' Merlin be the best lymers I've got," the old fellow said. John had told him why the hounds were required.

I pointed out the place near the Ladywell where Uctred's blood had stained the ground. The fewterer led his charges a few paces from the spot, for he did not want them to mark Uctred's scent rather than the felon's. He led the animals in a wide circle, and a few paces to the north the hounds grew excited, their noses twitching a few inches above the grass.

The fewterer said nothing, but made a motion with his hand and instantly the hounds were off, straining at their leashes. They led us a quarter-mile to the north, to the bank of Shill Brook. The stream is shallow there, little more than ankle deep. Here the spoor ended, and although we waded across the brook and the hounds searched to regain the trail, they were unable to do so.

Before I departed the castle Sunday evening I told Cicely Wagge to keep a cup or two of ale ready and if Uctred showed signs of waking she was to lift his head and see if he would drink. But she was not to give him food. Not yet, even if he regained his wits and asked. I did not know what organs the dagger might have damaged and did not want to discover some harm done to his gut by allowing him to eat.

I broke my fast Monday with half a maslin loaf and ale, and left Galen House for the castle before the second hour, as Adela appeared at the door. I was eager to learn how Uctred had fared overnight, and had tucked what I believed was his dagger in my belt, so that if he was alert I could ask him of it.

"'E awoke middle of the night," Cicely said, "so I give 'im some ale, like you said. Spilled most of it. Ain't woke up again."

I looked down on the sleeping man and even though the light was poor it seemed to me his face was not so pale, his lips not so tinged in blue. I drew back the blanket which covered him and inspected the wound. It no longer oozed blood. And although the edges of the cut were red, no pus flowed from around the sutures. I was well pleased.

I intended to request of John Chamberlain that he provide another retainer to watch over Uctred. Cicely had kept vigil through the night and would be fatigued. I told the woman of my plan, but she would not hear of it.

"Ain't tired," she said. "Just sat 'ere on this bench all night. Dozed some. When Uctred wakes 'e'll find a friend tendin' to 'im."

I agreed, told Cicely to send word to me as soon as there was any change, for good or ill, in Uctred's state, then turned to leave the guest chamber. Lord Gilbert entered as I did so.

"What news?" he said.

I told him of Cicely's report and the woman curtsied awkwardly as I did.

Perhaps it was the sound of voices after the silence of the night. I looked a last time at Uctred before I departed the chamber and saw his eyes blink open. My employer was also departing.

"Wait!" I shouted.

He did, glancing to me with one raised eyebrow, as he is inclined to do when puzzled.

"He wakes," I said, and hurried to the bed.

Uctred's eyes were now wide open. They followed me as I bent over him. In a hoarse whisper he said, "Thirsty."

I filled a cup with ale, lifted his head, and he managed to swallow nearly all. Only a few drops fell to his beard.

"Hurts," he then said.

Thirst I could deal with effectively. Pain was another matter. I had in my chest at Galen House herbs which may reduce a man's pain, but there is nothing in God's creation which will end pain completely. But for death.

"I will leave you for a time and get some physics which will dull your pain," I said. "I will return anon. Do you understand?"

Uctred nodded, then closed his eyes.

"We must ask who attacked him," Lord Gilbert said.

"He sleeps," I replied. "When I return with herbs I will awaken him. Mayhap then he will be able to answer."

I hurried to Galen House where I retrieved a pouch of crushed hemp seeds and another of the fresh-pounded willow bark. I saw questions in Kate's eyes, so briefly reviewed Uctred's condition for her, then hastened to the castle.

Uctred was yet sleeping when I entered the guest chamber. Cicely said he'd not awakened in the time I was away. Should I awaken him to give him herbs which would ease his pain? Whilst he slept he would not suffer. Waking him seemed pointless but for the possibility he might be able to identify his assailant.

If the man who stabbed Uctred was another of Lord Gilbert's retainers the man, if wounded in the fight with Uctred, might be identified by the fresh wound he bore. I sought Lord Gilbert, who had departed the guest chamber when I went to Galen House, and suggested a scheme whereby we might discover some lacerated page or groom or valet. Lord Gilbert agreed. His marshal, Sir William Daubney, would compel the grooms of the marshalsea to disrobe, then he would inspect their bodies for new wounds. John Chamberlain and the castle chaplain would require the same of all other of Lord Gilbert's male retainers. I did not believe it meet to demand the same of his female servants, and thought it unlikely a scullery maid would have attacked Uctred anyway.

This survey of castle inhabitants was completed within an hour. Not without some grumbling. Well, the day was chill. Sir William had just reported on the condition of his charges – all were unmarred – when there came a rapping upon the solar door. 'Twas Cicely with news of Uctred. He had awakened.

I hurried down the interior stairs to the guest chamber, with Lord Gilbert close behind. Uctred lay still under his blanket, the only sign of life his eyes, which followed us from the door to his bedside.

"I have physics for you," I said, "to ease your pain." The pouches of hemp seed and willow bark lay upon a table beside the ewer of ale and a cup. I poured a generous helping of each into the cup, filled it with ale, then took the brew to Uctred. I assisted him to raise his head and he emptied the cup in one draft.

"Do you remember what happened at the Ladywell?" Lord Gilbert said.

"Aye," Uctred croaked. "Stabbed."

"Who attacked you?"

"Don't know."

"You didn't see the man?"

"I did."

I held the dagger before his eyes. "Is this yours?"

Uctred blinked. "Aye."

"You saw the man who stabbed you?" Lord Gilbert said. "Who was it? I'll have the lout in the dungeon before dinner."

"Don't know," Uctred whispered. "Never seen 'im before."

"You were stabbed by a man not of Bampton?"

"Aye."

"Describe the fellow," I said.

Uctred took a deep breath, as if to steel himself for an ordeal. "Short. 'Bout as tall as me. Thin face. Beard beginnin' to grow gray. Wore a brown cotehardie. . . threadbare an' tattered." He fell silent, as if speaking these few words had been an effort beyond his strength.

"There was a trace of blood on your dagger when I found it near the Ladywell," I said. "Did you wound your attacker?"

"Tried to."

"You may have succeeded."

A man not of Bampton, nor of the Weald most likely, had struck down a retainer of one of the great barons of the realm. There is much danger in doing such a thing. A man would need great cause to risk such a perilous deed. The felon would know that Lord Gilbert was bound to take such an attack as a personal affront. And Uctred wore Lord Gilbert's livery of blue and black. No man familiar with Bampton could mistake Uctred for the servant of some other.

"You went to the Ladywell to beseech St. Frideswide for your vision?" I asked.

"Aye. Don't see so well. All folk say water from the well may cure."

I bent over Uctred, held a candle close, and studied his eyes. "You have cataracts," I told him. "They need couching."

"'Eard of that. Can it make me see clear again?"

"Sometimes. But often when 'tis done the patient requires lenses to see clearly."

"Where could I get 'em? Seen a monk at Eynsham Abbey once what 'ad 'em. Come from Italy an' cost three shillins."

Uctred had raised himself on an elbow during this exchange, but now fell back against his pillow. I had couched a monk's cataracts some years before, but the house he served could afford to purchase lenses for him. Would Lord Gilbert provide such for Uctred? Not likely if his finances were as tenuous as John Chamberlain believed. What, then, would be gained by speaking more of this to Uctred? Better to leave it be.

"Leave it be" – the words carved into Galen House door. Could this attack against Uctred have to do with my search for Edmund Harkins' slayer? I dismissed the thought. What possible connection could there be between the murder of a disliked villager and some unknown man stabbing Uctred?

Two years past a madman had run amuck in Abingdon, stabbing four folk on the street, one of whom perished, before he was subdued. Mayhap this had happened to Uctred. Had he been in the wrong place at the wrong time when some crazed man found him? Would a madman have wit to erase his trail by wading Shill Brook? Not likely. Then again, perhaps the felon waded the brook with no notion of obscuring his passing. Coincidence? Bailiffs do not believe in coincidence.

Responding to my questions had weakened Uctred. Or perhaps the crushed hemp seeds and pounded willow bark were taking effect. His eyes blinked shut and his breathing became measured, regular. He would live, I felt certain. But would he suffer lasting hurt from the wound? Of this I could not be sure.

I returned to Galen House for my dinner: aloes of lamb with wheaten loaves and parsley butter. As is her custom Bessie dominated the conversation and as is his custom John concentrated on his repast. Why waste time talking when a meal is before you?

I told Kate and Adela of Uctred's condition and his description of the attack and attacker.

"That account could fit half the tenants and villeins of the shire," Kate said. "Even to a tattered brown cotehardie."

"Indeed. But few such men will have a recent wound. And Uctred was sure he'd not seen the man before. I could require men of Bampton and the Weald to allow an inspection, to learn if any have a fresh laceration. But what would be the point? Uctred would have recognized a man of Bampton."

"Mayhap," Kate said.

"What do you mean?"

"He had been stabbed and was fighting for his life. Would that not make of him a poor witness?"

"It might," I agreed.

Kate's insight is often thoughtful, although in this case it created suspects where I had assumed there were none. I must ask Uctred again if he was sure he'd never seen his attacker before.

He was. Firmly so. I returned to the castle after dinner and asked him.

"Hungry," he said. I thought this a good sign, so sent Cicely to the kitchen for a wheaten loaf. I did not think Lord Gilbert would take offense if I provided Uctred with a loaf meant for his table. If Uctred could eat without doing harm to his wounded belly he should. Starvation never cured an illness nor healed an injury.

Cicely returned with the loaf and Uctred ate it all, then washed down the meal with a cup of ale laced with more willow bark and hemp seeds. He set the cup aside, belched, then winced. Pain is the body's way of telling a man that whatever he did to cause his discomfort he should not do again.

Frustration dogged my steps as I left the castle. I had had no success in discovering who slew Edmund Harkins and now had an obligation to seek the man who had tried to slay Uctred. I could not see any greater success in exposing the latter felony than the former.

I had told Cicely to send a page to me if there was any change in Uctred's condition, or if he asked for me because of some new recollection. I was of two minds regarding the possible appearance of a castle page. On the one hand it might mean Uctred had remembered something of his attacker which could lead to the man. On the other hand the approach of a page might mean Uctred had suffered a relapse; that consuming a loaf had done harm rather than good.

I walked Bampton's streets, observing folk as they went about their business. All seemed well, yet I sensed an undercurrent of unease. Was I the only town resident who did so? I stopped at the bridge over Shill Brook to gaze into the flowing stream. The rippling water offered no insight.

People were beginning to seek their homes as the sun dropped below the forest to the west. I did likewise. Adela was away to her home in the Weald. Christopher, Kate said, seemed quite pleased with his duty. I hoped the lad was not too pleased.

"I purchased fresh ale today," Kate said. "I saw that Maud Baker had raised a basket on a pole before her door. Leuca was there with two others," she continued. "They were in conversation on the street, their heads close together, but when they saw me approach, they ended their chat and hurried away. Will it be like this for ever? No women of the town will speak to me."

I saw a tear form in the corner of her eye. That men of Bampton avoided me did not trouble me much. Bailiffs are accustomed to being shunned. Our duties make us unpopular. But Kate had always enjoyed conversation with other women of Bampton. Call it gossip if you will, but what she learned she would relate to me and I often found the information useful.

But since I had begun to search for Edmund Harkins' slayer women of Bampton had been silent when Kate appeared.

Tuesday dawned grey and damp, matching my mood. I sat in the kitchen, near the fire, and consumed half a maslin loaf and a cup of the fresh ale. I needed to visit the castle and learn how Uctred fared but procrastinated until Adela arrived at the second hour. If the lass could tolerate the misty morning so could I. I greeted her, kissed Kate, and set off for the castle.

I was pleased to find Uctred alert and consuming another of Lord Gilbert's wheaten loaves, this one with a thick layer of parsley butter. The groom grinned at me when he saw me enter the guest chamber, and licked his lips. He did not show any sign of being in pain.

"I give you good day," I said, and seeing Uctred's answering smile my melancholy lifted. I began to believe that he would make a good recovery. "Are you in pain this morning?" I asked.

"Not so long as I lay still. Do I shift myself, me side aches. So I lay quiet, like. Got to rise to use the chamber pot, which ain't much fun. Teach me to pay more attention when I visit the Ladywell."

"Indeed. Have you cast your mind back to Sunday and the attack?"

"Aye, think on little else."

"Do you recall any more about the scoundrel who pierced you?"

"Nay. . . why would a man do so? I've done no harm to any man. Well, not lately. Gettin' too old to pick quarrels. Can't make sense of it."

"Men do not hide in ambush, waiting to slay another, for no reason," I said.

"You think I angered some man an' don't know it?"

"Mayhap. If we can find the man we will then find the reason. Or discover the reason and that will lead us to the villain. So continue to cast your mind back over the past month or so. See if you can pull from your memory an event now forgotten which might have angered some other."

"I will do so," Uctred said. "But truth is it ain't only me eyes which is gone bad. Don't remember things. Set off for the marshalsea a few days past an' when I got there couldn't remember why I'd done so."

I left Uctred in Cicely's capable care and departed the castle. The misty rain had ceased and an occasional patch of blue sky appeared, scudding rapidly between broken clouds. I decided to once again visit the shallow grave where pigs had discovered Edmund Harkins. I cannot say why. 'Twas a measure of my vacuous state that I could think of no other way to seek Edmund's slayer than to study once again the place where he had been found.

I was not the only man to consider doing so. I saw the holy man standing before his hut as I came near. He greeted me with a knuckle to his forehead and I asked if any others had visited the place where Edmund's corpse was found.

He shook his head.

"I am going there," I said, "to see if some evidence might have been overlooked."

The holy man pointed in the direction of the grave, then to himself.

"You have recently searched the place?" I asked.

He nodded.

"But found nothing?"

He shook his head, then pointed to me and back to himself.

"You will accompany me?"

He smiled and nodded.

Together we followed the obscure trail through the wood, our shoes and chauces becoming quite soaked by the time we reached the depression, now filling with fallen leaves, where Edmund had lain.

A thick layer of oak and beech leaves covered the ground, so that if any evidence of murder was here it was camouflaged. And had been when the corpse was first found, although the leafy covering was now thicker. I began to think this visit a fool's errand. What could be discovered now which was not found eleven days past?

With my toe I began to kick leaves away from the hole. This, of course, made for a thicker layer a few paces beyond the pit, and further dampened my shoes. The holy man saw, and began to also kick leaves aside. We soon had the space around the grave cleared of most leaves for three or four paces.

The button was of bone, and of aged tan color. 'Tis a wonder I noticed it where it lay in the decay of the forest floor. It was about an inch in diameter, perhaps a little more, and plain, without decoration. The commons wear buttons such as this to close cotehardies and houpelands and tunics and such. Gentlemen and ladies will use buttons of brass or pewter or even silver – Lord Gilbert does – or have buttons of bone carved into decorative patterns. Here was a button some tenant or villein had made for his own use. 'Twas not even cut to a perfect circle, but was slightly oval in shape. Two small holes in the center showed where thread had fastened the button to a garment. This was possibly why it had torn free. Most folk make their buttons with three or four holes.

Why would a man lose a button here, in a wood? Was he poaching Lord Gilbert's deer? Or did he have a more sinister reason for being here? Was the cotehardie of one of Edmund Harkins' slayers now missing a button? Perhaps it had been, but was no longer. The button was crude and a replacement could be made in an hour or so, if the materials were at hand. Should I seek a man in Bampton who wore a garment missing a button? What other clue did I have?

The holy man watched me as I studied the button, then held out his hand in a request to examine the bone. This he did, shrugged and handed it back. I believe he thought, as I, that this was quite inconsequential evidence. Nevertheless, evidence it was.

My stomach told me 'twas time for dinner. I bade the holy man good day, placed the bone button in my pouch, and set off for Galen House. Kate and Adela had prepared fraunt hemelle. As we ate I told Kate of revisiting Edmund's temporary grave and the discovery of the button. I drew it from my pouch and gave it to her for inspection.

"A young man," she said.

"How so?"

"The elderly do not hold with new fashions."

This is true, and buttons have been in common use but for a short time. My father refused to don a buttoned cotehardie.

"An old man," Kate continued, "will not want a snug cotehardie which will display his paunch. He will prefer something loose, which he can draw over his head. So what need of buttons?"

"And old men are not likely to slay one another," I added, "or prowl the forest seeking Lord Gilbert's deer."

"What will you do now?" Kate asked.

"I will walk the town seeking some man whose garment is missing a button."

"What of some woman?"

"Would a woman have slain Edmund, or be roaming the forest to poach a deer?"

"Not likely," Kate said.

Chapter 10

I was surprised that so many folk of Bampton wore garments missing a button. One man in ten, and women also, was without at least one button. Most were apparently buttons of wood, judging by the buttons remaining. Wooden buttons, I think, may split and fall away. Bone is more durable. Nevertheless I saw a half-dozen or so men wearing garments which had lost a bone button. And these were buttons close in size to the one in my pouch.

Had a chance discovery whittled down the number of suspects in the slaying of Edmund Harkins? Surely more than six men of Bampton wore garments fastened with bone buttons. How many more had I not seen this day? And how many of these had lost a button?

Kate spoke true. Nearly all of the men I saw who wore buttoned cotehardies were young, no matter if the buttons were of wood or bone. Oddly enough, although the holy man saw men entering the Weald late one night when Edmund had gone missing, which I felt certain had to do with his death, I saw but one man of the Weald who wore bone buttons and none of his were missing. Folk of the Weald tend to be less prosperous than residents of Bampton. Therefore those who closed garments with buttons used wooden.

At supper that evening Kate asked to once again inspect the button. She turned it in her fingers whilst Bessie chattered and John ignored all but his pottage.

I broke my fast next morning with half a loaf and ale. No butter. 'Twas a fast day. Days were growing short, so when Adela arrived at the second hour the sky was yet pale. The lass was breathless, as if she'd trotted from the Weald, and after she entered she paused and glanced over her shoulder toward the shadowed street. Had Father Harold taken to following Adela in the morning now that she was escorted in the afternoon?

When the lass passed into the kitchen I looked up and down the street from Galen House door but saw only the distant shape of a fleshy matron setting off on her morning business. 'Twas surely not the young priest, and I saw no others about. What did Adela fear? Or was I making too much of her apparent timidity?

I was pleased with Uctred's fettle. He was munching another of Lord Gilbert's fine wheaten loaves and enjoying it so much I thought it possible he might claim a continued bellyache so as to remain an invalid in the guest chamber.

"Thought of somethin' since you was last 'ere," he said. "The rogue what struck me down limped."

"Mayhap when you bloodied your dagger fighting back you struck him in the leg," I said.

"Nay. 'E'd turned 'is back to flee, so I slashed at 'is back. Didn't know I'd wounded 'im 'til you told me of blood on me dagger. Thought I'd just ripped through 'is cotehardie."

"So when he ran off he limped? Badly?"

"Nay. Must be why I'd not remembered 'til now. Hardly noticeable. Didn't slow 'im down much."

"I've come to inspect your wound," I said. "Is the ache worse or better than two days past?"

"'Bout the same. Tender to touch... so I don't."

I drew back the blanket and raised Uctred's kirtle. What I saw worried me. The wound itself was not issuing pus, although the stitched closure was red, but the surrounding flesh was swollen and warm to the touch.

Uctred apparently saw my concern. "You ain't 'appy?" he said.

"The cut has festered, I fear. On the surface all is well, but within your gut is some purulence. Do you see blood when you pass water?"

"Aye. Pinkish, like."

"Is there more color today than yesterday?"

Uctred pursed his lips. "Nay, I'd say not."

"Less?"

"Aye. Mayhap some."

I had done all I knew for the man. A wound to the belly is often fatal. All depends upon which organs have been pierced. Could Uctred survive if his bladder was holed, or a kidney? Blood in his urine suggested that one of these organs had been harmed. My year of study at Paris had not taught the repair of such viscera, for the good reason that no such mending is possible. If a man's abdomen is opened he will likely perish. I did not say this to Uctred and, indeed, I remained hopeful that his wound would heal with no further action from me, for there was nothing more I could do for the man but pray the Lord Christ would intercede beyond my skills.

What was I to do now concerning Uctred's assailant? Walk Bampton's streets seeking men who limped? I'd already circled the town casting about for men who'd lost a button. I knew of several men who limped. Giles Elton was born with a foot turned in and hobbles through his day. He would not have attacked Uctred and then run away. The man can barely walk.

Alan Hutter is another matter. He limps some, not badly, and could surely run. The first year I was in Bampton Alan was working a saw pit and the log he and another were raising slipped from the scaffold and crushed his foot. I set the broken bones with a plaster as best I could, but I was new at the business of surgery at the time, and even had I been experienced there are in a man's foot so many small bones that putting them right so they knit properly is nearly impossible.

One would not have to walk Bampton's streets long before observing men and women whose arthritic joints cause them pain so they totter about. Could any of these run if necessary? Mayhap. What was I to do? Challenge every man I saw limping to run, to learn if he could do so?

"Do you suppose," Kate said as we sat to our dinner, "that the button you found belonged not to one of Edmund Harkins' slayers, but to Edmund?"

"The thought had occurred to me, but I cannot see why it would have torn free."

"Mayhap he was yet alive when taken to the wood and struggled against his adversaries. Or the button was ripped away when men lifted him, then dropped him in the grave."

"There is a way to know," I said. "I will take the button to Leuca. She may recognize it if it was from Edmund's cotehardie."

"How does Uctred?" she asked.

I told her of his claim that his assailant had limped as he ran from the Ladywell.

"So you need to find a man who can run, but not well, and likely suffers discomfort when so doing," Kate concluded.

"Aye, that sums up the matter."

"Bampton is becoming a place of murder and mayhem," Kate said with a shudder.

"Until a few weeks past the town was at peace. Then Edmund was slain, a new and troublesome priest arrived, and Uctred was attacked."

"Could these events be tied together in some way?" Kate mused.

"I cannot see how. That all of these lamentable incidents have occurred near to the same time is, it seems to me, but coincidence."

"I have heard you say that bailiffs do not believe in coincidence."

"True. And because I cannot see how these deplorable events fit together does not mean they do not. It may mean I have not the wit to see the pattern."

During this conversation Adela was silent, listening, consuming her dinner. When she spoke I was startled. She was usually silent at dinner.

"That priest," she said softly, "sent 'is clerk to me father yesterday."

"For what purpose?" I said, although I knew at least the rudiments of the visit.

"Father 'arold will raise Father's rent if I will not come to serve as 'is 'ousekeeper."

"How much of the bishop's lands does your father possess?"

"Two strips. Quarter yardland or thereabouts. Clerk told Father I've got 'til Sunday."

"What rent does your father now pay?"

"Don't know."

"I will speak to Father Thomas about this. It is good you brought it to me. Do not fear that you will be forced to go to Father Harold."

I hoped I was not promising more than I could deliver, and that Sir Jaket would hurry.

Following dinner I set off for Rosemary Lane. Leuca had prepared a simple pottage for her family as 'twas a fast day. But fast day or not, likely a simple pottage served for every meal.

I produced the bone button from my pouch and showed it to Leuca. The woman seemed to recoil, but quickly caught herself, as if she understood that she had given something away. What? She had, I thought, seen this button or one very much like it before.

When I asked her about it she claimed no knowledge. "Edmund 'ad wooden buttons 'e made 'imself. Like these." She pointed to the buttons which closed her cotehardie. They were tolerably well made, and would serve as well as any made of bone, but without the prestige.

Leuca did not say more, nor did she ask why I had questioned her about the button. I thought this a remarkable lack of curiosity. Unless she already knew, or guessed, whose button it was and where I'd found it.

For want of anything more pressing to do I set off for the castle to learn how Uctred fared. As the visit was not urgent I paused upon the bridge over Shill Brook and watched the current. From the corner of my eye I saw movement, turned, and saw Leuca hurriedly disappear beyond the corner of Rosemary Lane and the High Street. Where might the woman be going in such haste? And did that haste have to do with my visit? Mayhap I am too suspicious. Bailiffs tend to become so. There are few naive bailiffs. Those who are soon find themselves seeking other employment.

I departed the bridge, curious as to where Leuca may have gone, but when I passed the curve in the High Street she was nowhere to be seen. Did she go to warn some man that I had found his missing button?

I decided to hide myself and wait for her return. I concealed myself behind a grove of mulberry bushes, expecting her speedy return. She had left her children at home alone. Half an hour later she had still not reappeared and I was about to quit my hideout. But as I did I saw the woman. She carried two loaves. She had visited the baker. In the afternoon? When his oven was cooling? And in such haste? She showed no sign of being in a hurry to return to Rosemary Lane. Did it take half an hour to purchase two loaves? Mayhap she had enjoyed some gossip with Maud.

Uctred's abdomen was yet swollen and tender, but he claimed that when he had last passed water there was less blood than in the morning. The presence of blood where it should not be is always troubling, so less of it in such a place is a good thing.

I had not forgotten Adela's quandary. From the castle I went to Father Thomas's vicarage. His clerk was about to walk to Galen House to escort the lass to her home. It was clear that he did not find the obligation onerous.

"How may I serve you?" the priest said as Christopher trotted off for Church View Street.

"Father Harold's clerk, Randall Creten, has told Stephen Parkin that his rent will be raised if Adela will not become Father Harold's housekeeper. The man has not two pennies to rub together as it is."

"Bah! The man believes that as he is Bishop Brantyngham's nephew he can disregard me and Father Ralph. Christopher!" the priest called after his departing clerk.

The lad hurried back to the vicarage.

"When you have seen Adela safely home tell her father he may ignore the threat Randall made."

The lad seemed puzzled, not knowing what threat had been made, or why. But he had been instructed to do a thing, and as it involved Adela was pleased to do it.

"When was it Sir Jaket took Lord Gilbert's letter to the bishop?" the priest asked.

"He and Thomas and Richard departed Saturday morning. He should be near to Exeter by now, or mayhap even there."

"We may receive the bishop's decision by, say, Sunday or Monday, think you?"

"Mayhap."

"Cannot come too soon."

"You wish to be rid of Father Harold?"

"You know well the answer to that. Although no more than you, I think."

"We are assuming the bishop will do as Lord Gilbert asks," I said.

"Why would he not? To remove Father Harold and replace him will cause him no hardship, whereas to defy such a peer as Lord Gilbert will surely have adverse effects for his position. The new archbishop, whomever he may be, might be persuaded to send an archdeacon to investigate the finances of the diocese of Exeter."

"Hah. A thing no bishop would welcome."

"Indeed," Father Thomas agreed.

"Tell me immediately if Randall is sent to Stephen again. Adela might not speak of it unless asked."

"Be assured I will ask," I said.

Thursday morning Adela arrived shortly before the second hour, shook water from her threadbare cloak and, as before, glanced back out of the door. So did I. She had not been followed. Evidently neither Father Harold nor his clerk thought pursuing the lass was worth rising early from bed on a damp morning.

"I 'eard Christopher say to my father what Father Thomas told 'im," Adela said. "'E is much relieved."

He would be. Since parliament decreed the Statute of Laborers it is against the law for a tenant to leave his lord's manor for the purpose of securing land at a lesser rent, and also a violation for a lord to tempt tenants to move to his fief by reducing rents. But plague has come and come again and many laborers have died. Gentlemen find workers hard to come by. Father Harold would risk losing a tenant did he raise Stephen Parkin's rent too much. He knew this, surely, for the Statute of Laborers is widely scorned.

I decided that I would visit Maud Baker to learn what I might of her chat with Leuca. Leuca Harkins had spent half an hour in purchasing two loaves. The exchange likely included some village gossip. And Leuca's surreptitious haste after our conversation was curious.

When Edmund first went missing Leuca seemed much distressed. That sentiment did not last. Within days after he was found she was about her business and appearing untroubled by her loss. Was she, when he was newly missing, but a credible player? Perhaps Maud could answer this question.

Robert Baker's oven was hot when I arrived, and business was good. Folk arrived every few minutes with pence and farthings, and departed with fresh loaves. 'Twas difficult to find a moment to speak to Maud, especially as the woman was busy at her vat, brewing fresh ale.

When customers thinned I approached Maud. She no doubt wondered why the town bailiff was lingering about her home. I enlightened her.

"Yesterday Leuca Harkins came here and bought two loaves. What conversation passed between you two?"

"Conversation? None. Bought the loaves from Robert, didn't she."

"And spent half an hour talking to your husband? I think not. What did you speak of?"

"I told you, Leuca spoke only to Robert."

"Mayhap 'tis time I took more interest in your brewing. The last ewer Kate purchased seemed thin. Have you begun watering your ale? Lord Gilbert would be displeased."

My employer has set a fine of six pence for any who brew and sell watered ale. Maud had never been assigned this penalty, not that she never watered her ale, but she'd not been caught out.

Margaret Bray, on the other hand, has been fined several times for watering her ale. But what is a penalty of six pence when balanced against a gain of perhaps twelve pence? Margaret will continue the practice so long as profit exceeds expense. The wonder is that many folk continue to purchase ale from her and others who also practice deceit. True, they charge less for ale than does Maud. And no wonder.

"You threaten me?" Maud said.

"Nay. I show you the times. Evil lurks in Bampton. Lord Gilbert employs me to root it out."

"Mayhap the evil you seek is not the evil you will find."

"What evil do I seek?"

"All of Bampton know you seek for those who slew Edmund Harkins."

"Indeed. Is there a second evil I may discover whilst uncovering the first?"

"There are many evils hidden in men's hearts."

"True. Most known only to the Lord Christ, and which He will deal with. But some wrongs must be righted in this life, else men will do wickedness fearing no consequences. So long as evils remain hid in men's hearts I have no responsibility. When the evil is no longer hid Lord Gilbert demands I act. So I say again, what did you and Leuca discuss?"

Maud turned away, placed two small logs under her steaming copper cauldron, then spoke. "Wants fresh ale, does Leuca, when this batch is ready."

"It took half an hour to tell you that?" I said. "And if you've only today begun, 'twill be two days before this ale can be sold. Will she drink water from Shill Brook or the well 'til then?"

"Guess so. Or buy from Margaret Bray."

"And you spoke of nothing else?"

The woman knew that I would not believe – did not believe – that a discussion of when this next batch of ale would be ready would take half an hour.

"Some town gossip," she finally said.

"Enlighten me."

"You be bailiff. 'Tis your business to know such matters."

"Indeed. So tell me what passes from wife to wife so I may better conduct my business."

Maud hesitated, considering, I think, whether or not she could be in trouble for speaking, or in more trouble for not speaking. She resolved the matter, and spoke.

"Leuca told me that one of Lord Gilbert's household knights has taken a message to the bishop."

How would Leuca know this, I wondered? And did she know what the letter contained?

"Three retainers, actually," I said. "Sir Jaket Bec, his squire, and also Lord Gilbert's son, Richard. Did Leuca tell you the subject of the message?"

"Didn't know, did she."

"I'd wager she shared a guess with you, or a rumor she'd heard."

Another silence while Maud stirred her vat and considered how much she need say to satisfy me. "Somethin' 'bout the new vicar," she said.

"And what might that be?"

"Lord Gilbert wants 'im gone, she's 'eard."

"Heard where? How?"

"Didn't say."

"Was she pleased?"

"Oh, aye. Most folks is."

"Why is that?"

I had my own reasons for wishing Father Harold inflicted upon some other parish but did not know other Bampton residents agreed with the sentiment. Here was another matter folk of the town did not share with me. What good is a bailiff whose ear is deaf to the talk of his lord's tenants?

"Rather not say, an' you don't mind," Maud said.

"If I do mind will you speak?"

"Don't want no trouble."

"You will be in trouble if you tell me what you know touching Father Harold's standing with your neighbors? Trouble with who? The priest? Me? Lord Gilbert? Father Thomas or Father Ralph?"

What could the new priest have done to offend his parishioners of which I had no knowledge? Did they know of his designs on Adela? They would be furious if they did. If a woman wished to live with a priest of her own volition, and many did, few would question her choice. But for a priest to coerce a maid would anger his flock. He is to be their shepherd, not the wolf at the fold.

"Father Harold don't keep silent of what folks confess," Maud said, "an' I'll say no more."

"He has bandied about what some townsman has confessed?"

"I'll say no more."

If the priest did such a thing what reason could he have? Might it profit him to spread abroad what he was required to conceal? Or would he profit simply by a threat to expose what he knew? Either was a flagrant abuse of his post.

"Whose confession has been violated?" I asked.

"I'll say no more."

I believed her. Her voice and features were resolute and she attacked her brewing barley with the stirring stick 'til I thought the liquid might overflow the cauldron and quench her fire.

Here was a matter for Father Thomas. I bade Maud and Robert good day, and set off for Galen House and my dinner. I would seek Father Thomas with a full belly.

Chapter 11

Kate and Adela had roasted a capon and added maslin loaves and parsley butter to the meal. I was well content and prepared to live at peace with all men when I had eaten my fill. Peace can be difficult to come by unless a man is prepared to allow evil to flourish with no opposition. Conflict may betimes become a duty to justice, for peace and justice are not synonymous. Perhaps this is why the Lord Christ said He did come not to bring peace but a sword. Justice requires, upon occasion, the use of a sword.

Casting aside my desire to live at peace with all men I complimented Kate and Adela upon the meal and set off for Father Thomas's vicarage, where I would find strife. Find it or create it.

Father Thomas was licking his chops, having just finished his dinner. He was, he told me, on his way to the church, and a moment later I heard the church bell ring calling folk to the noon Angelus.

I followed the priest to St. Beornwald's, waited while he completed the devotional, then met him in the porch. I wasted no time in pleasantries but went straight to the point. Father Thomas's eyes grew wide as I recounted Maud Baker's accusation – without naming the woman. He did not, I think, believe the charge. Not at first.

"What evidence did the woman supply," he asked when I'd finished the tale, "that this misconduct has truly happened?"

"I could not pry that from her. She spoke the complaint, then said she would say no more."

"She did not name the person whose confession Father Harold has betrayed?"

"Nay."

"Then how do we know 'tis so? No man has complained to me of this sacrilege – neither the man whose confession has been transgressed nor others who may have heard of it."

"Have you known Maud Baker to be a faithless woman?" I said.

"Maud is the woman who told of this? Nay, she has always seemed truthful."

"'Tis my belief that Father Harold is using some man's confession against him, and Maud has learned of it. But few others. If Father Harold's transgression became widely known his reputation would suffer for it. How then could he bend the confessor to his purpose by requiring something of the man under the threat of making the sin known to the town?"

"Hmm. Aye. Father Harold could not hold a man to his will by threatening to make public what all men already know."

"Precisely. This is why neither you, nor I, nor most others of Bampton have heard of it."

"But the person whose confession has been violated has spoken to Maud of it, you think?"

"Aye. Or some other who is a close friend of both."

"Will you seek to discover who that might be?"

"I have already to learn who murdered Edmund Harkins and tried to slay Uctred. Seems to me you and Father Ralph should seek out the man whose confession is betrayed."

"Man?"

"You think 'tis a woman's confession Father Harold heard and is now using against her?"

"Would a man," Father Thomas said, "unburden himself to Maud Baker?"

"Not likely. But he might complain to his wife of Father Harold's betrayal and she has sought comfort from Maud. Misery loves company."

"So it is said," the priest agreed. "And I grant you the assertion. So we really cannot know whether Father Harold's treachery involves a man or a woman."

"Nay. Let us hope Sir Jaket will return soon with a letter from the bishop which will send Father Harold on his way."

"Maud Baker would not speak to you of what Father Harold's deceit encompassed," Father Thomas said, "but will she speak of it to another? Mayhap the wives of Bampton will soon know a thing of which you and I will be ignorant."

"Ignorance may be no bad thing?"

"True. If I knew what may happen tomorrow I might draw a blanket over my head in the morning and remain abed."

"On the other hand, someone may have confessed to Father Harold of matters involving Edmund's death or the attack against Uctred," I said. "And chose the new priest to hear his confession because he is new."

"Mayhap. Although what difference that would make to a guilty man I cannot guess."

"Or a guilty woman."

"Would a woman strike down Edmund?"

"She might if he beat her regularly."

Father Thomas stared at me. "You suspect Leuca did away with her husband?"

"I suspect no one. I suspect everyone."

"But for a wife to slay her husband is considered treason. The punishment is hanging, or being burnt alive. Would a wife risk that?"

"Might depend," I replied, "upon what she risks if her husband remains alive."

"Hmm. Just so. I must speak to Father Ralph of what you have told me. Mayhap we can put our heads together and ferret out what Father Harold is up to."

"Be cautious. If it should happen that Lord Gilbert's request to the bishop is denied and Father Harold remains in Bampton, his wrath will be great. We would all suffer, but especially you and Father Ralph if he suspects you have conspired against him. Bishop Brantyngham might send you to another parish and replace you with lackeys."

"You are not confident of Lord Gilbert's influence?"

"There is a new archbishop. Until Simon Langham tests the wind, he may be hesitant to perturb a bishop."

"He may also desire good standing with Lord Gilbert," Father Thomas said. "A man new to such an office must tread a fine line."

"Aye. Many bishops desired the post, I'm sure. Some may be pleased they did not gain it, and may now live out their lives in obscurity."

"As obscure as a bishop may be," Father Thomas chuckled. "If a bishop genuinely seeks obscurity he will resign his post and take vows, becoming a brother in some monastery."

"Hah. Where he may then trouble abbot and prior, no doubt. When a man has held the reins of power I suspect he finds it difficult to give them up."

"As will Father Harold," Father Thomas said. "If he has power due to misuse of the confessional over some man or woman, he may seek to enlarge it. Much hinges upon his uncle's decision."

"To what purpose, I wonder, would Father Harold hold a man's confession hostage?"

"He seeks some gain, to be sure," Father Thomas said.

"Coins? Of what use are pennies and groats to a priest?"

"He may wish to light his chamber with silver candlesticks, or dine from plate, using silver spoons."

"'Twill not improve his meal nor provide better light to own either," I replied.

"Just so. But when do most men decide they have enough of this world's goods?"

"Never. The man with one yardland wants two, the wife with six hens wants a dozen, the gentleman with three palfreys wants an ambler also.

"What penance would you require if a man confessed to you that he had slain another?" I continued.

"Pilgrimage, and an arduous one. To Compostela, barefoot."

"And would that allow a man to escape hell and see heaven when he dies?"

"Surely. Did not the Lord Christ tell St. Peter that whatever he bound on earth would be bound in heaven, and whatever he loosed on earth would be loosed in heaven?"

"Do His words to St. Peter apply also to you?"

"Certainly. Pope Gregory is the inheritor of that trust, and we who are ordained share the warrant."

"The Lord Christ also said 'twould be difficult for a rich man to enter heaven," I said. "Who is richer than the Pope?"

The priest was silent for a moment. "Very few," he conceded.

"Then we are required to obey a man who may be bound for hell?"

"You tread dangerous ground, Sir Hugh."

"Father Harold will not hear of this conversation, will he?"

"Nay, not from me."

"To change the subject, if some man suddenly leaves Bampton for an extended pilgrimage, may we know then who murdered Edmund Harkins?"

"You asked what penance I would require. I cannot speak for Father Harold. Especially if he has broken the seal of confession. Mayhap his purpose, if he did this evil thing, will in time become clear."

"Let us hope he will be gone before that time appears," I said.

I departed the porch and left Father Thomas to ponder what he had learned. I was halfway down Church View Street to Galen House and saw he had not yet passed under the lychgate.

Kate's appetite having returned, she consumed a substantial portion of the ravioles which she and Adela had prepared before the lass departed for the Weald in company with Christopher.

"Adela seems relieved that her father will not be penalized for her refusal to serve Father Harold," Kate said.

"Serve" was a euphemism for what the priest really wanted. Kate thought the truth too harsh for Bessie's tender years. I agreed.

"For the past weeks," Kate continued, "Adela has been somber and reticent. She goes about her duties well enough, but never speaks of gossip from the Weald as she once did. Today, however, she said a curious thing.

She said that her mother would not see another suffer injustice and remain passive."

"Her mother? She did not say this of her father?"

"Nay. And when she had spoken she turned from me and covered her mouth. As if she had said a thing unintended."

"What preceded this assertion?"

"I was speaking of my own mother. 'Twas eighteen years ago on this date when she perished of plague. I was old enough that I remember her very well, and spoke of her virtues as we worked. Adela, I think, wished to praise her mother as I did mine."

"'Tis indeed praiseworthy for a woman, or a man, to oppose injustice," I said. "But why, I wonder, would Adela act as if she had spoken unwisely? You are sure her behavior indicated that she rued her words?"

"Aye. Why would the lass regret praising her mother? 'Twas a puzzle to me then," Kate said, "and remains so. Mayhap I saw some remorse where none was."

"Mayhap," I agreed. But my Kate is observant, and I harbored the thought that Adela's reticence in the past weeks had to do with more than Father Harold's unwanted attention. Might her conduct have to do with Edmund Harkins' death? If so, how, and did I want to know?

Must a bailiff always act upon what he has learned? Might I know a thing and bury it in the recesses of my mind? Such concealed knowledge has a way of rising to the surface, like froth on a cup of ale. Usually in the middle of the night, when I am alone with my thoughts. Sometimes they are pleasant company, sometimes not. Disagreeable thoughts cannot be dispelled. The more I try not to think on a thing the more likely I am to do so.

My intentions were good. I sought a man's killer. But are good intentions enough? And must they always be acted upon? Is it better to have good intentions not carried out, or to have no good intentions at all? The result will be the same. Mayhap.

I tried not to think on these matters that night in our bed, but of course could then think of nothing else. 'Tis not possible to unthink a thing. Like trying to unremember a matter one would like to forget. Kate, I was pleased to observe, slept soundly. She was making another human in God's image, and needed her rest.

Friday dawned clear and sun-filled. The sky in Britain is occasionally clear and blue. My thoughts did not emulate the unobscured heavens. I may have slept some brief time during the night, but if so I could not remember. Of course, if a man sleeps he remembers nothing of it but the occasional dream. I digress.

The sky was bright and cheering but my mood was not. I was learning things which brought dolor rather than joy. People of Bampton, some at least, seemed to prefer I not discover who had slain Edmund Harkins. The town was cursed with a deceitful priest. Uctred would recover or not, and nothing I could do would change his future. What I could do for him I had already done, except discover his assailant and see the man before the King's Eyre. But that would do nothing to heal Uctred's wound.

Thoughts of Uctred caused me to seek the castle after I broke my fast. I went there apprehensive of what I would find. It seemed to me Uctred would heal and his health improve every day, or I would find him weaker and nearer to meeting the Lord Christ. His condition would not remain as 'twas. It would improve or he would fail, but not remain as he was. Of course, all men are a day nearer to meeting the Lord Christ when they awaken each morning. I desire such a day. But not yet. Nor, I suspect, did Uctred.

I found Uctred alone in the guest chamber. He was awake, alert, and saw the question in my eyes.

"Cicely's gone for ale an' a loaf. An' I told 'er to seek 'er own bed at night. Them physics you give me help me sleep the night. No sense in 'er sittin' 'ere listenin' to me snore."

Was Uctred stronger than yesterday? Aye. For this I was much pleased and breathed a silent prayer that saints and angels would continue to intercede for the man. No man lives for ever, but I was becoming confident that this wound would not send Uctred to the churchyard. Some other injury or malady would, but that was for another day, another worry.

The hinges to the door of the guest chamber squealed and Cicely entered bearing a loaf and a large pewter tankard. A shadow darkened the door behind her. This figure stepped into the chamber, and light from the window illuminated the fellow. 'Twas Arthur, I thought, returned from the dead!

The youth was the image of Arthur. Or would have been when Arthur was twenty years old. His face was unlined and nearly beardless, but the features were Arthur's. The body also. The lad was almost as tall as me, but weighed at least four stone more. He had nearly to turn sideways to pass through the doorway, so broad were his shoulders. His legs were thick and short. I have in the past described Arthur as resembling a wine cask set upon two coppiced stumps. The description suited the son also.

"Here is Janyn Wagge," Cicely said, "come from Goodrich to serve Lord Gilbert at Bampton."

The lad tugged a forelock and smiled. 'Twas Arthur's smile.

"I am pleased to meet you," I said. "Your father and I had many adventures together."

"I've 'eard of some," Janyn said.

There was regular movement of retainers between Bampton and Goodrich. When Lord Gilbert traveled there for the winter, which he would soon do, he took a few grooms and valets. Many of these accompanied him to Pembroke when he chose to reside there. Gossip found opportunity to travel from one castle to another. How much, I wondered, of what Janyn had heard was truth, and how much had been embellished in the telling? If the lad remained in service to Lord Gilbert in Bampton I would likely find an answer to that question.

Cicely gave the loaf to Uctred and placed the tankard upon a table within his reach. I was pleased to see him tear chunks from the loaf and devour them voraciously. I asked of blood in his urine, and between bites he replied that there was yet some sign, but not so much as days past. This was welcome news.

Folk who dine at Lord Gilbert's high table on fast days will consume fish of various types prepared with savory sauces. His grooms and valets and pages, however, will content themselves with pottage of peas or beans flavored with leeks and onions. I thought Uctred's convalescence would be speeded if he could have a piece of fish for his dinner. So I told Cicely to tell the cook that Sir Hugh prescribed a portion of pike or halibut or mussels. Whatever would grace Lord Gilbert's trencher. Uctred heard, and smiled in anticipation.

I was not eager to leave a place where I had found success to visit some other place where I had failed. And that place of failure was wherever I might go in Bampton or the Weald. I could not hide in Uctred's chamber all day, however, so bade him, Cicely, and Janyn good day, and set off to seek a felon.

My problem was that I knew and liked nearly all of the town's residents. True, I had not liked Edmund, but he had not slain himself. Of the men of Bampton and the Weald there was not one I thought capable of murder. There had been such men in the past, but such rogues had done evil, been found out and punished, or died of some natural cause, so that now Bampton seemed blessedly free of scoundrels. This troubled me. When, if, I discovered who had slain Edmund 'twould be some fellow I liked who would be condemned.

And the guilty man would probably be popular in the town. For uncovering his sin I would not be. Would I be respected? Is it possible for a bailiff to be both popular and respected? Probably. It is certainly possible to be unpopular and disrespected. If I became so, my value to Lord Gilbert would end. This was not a prospect I wished to consider.

I wandered across the bridge over Shill Brook with no destination in mind. Where Rosemary Lane joins the High Street I glanced back over my shoulder and saw a man standing in Leuca Harkins' toft, talking to her. He was unfamiliar. The vultures, I thought, were beginning to circle. Leuca would not like to be compared to dead meat. All analogies eventually break down.

The man was not of Bampton or the Weald. News traveled fast, I thought. Some man of Lew or Shilton or other nearby town had learned of an available widow in Bampton and come calling. He would have plenty of local competition when a respectable time had passed. And mayhap the time would not be respectable as suitors saw their courtship failing if they waited too long to make intentions known to Leuca.

I had little interest in the men who might be attracted to Leuca, so continued on my way, past Robert Baker's oven, to St. Andrew's Chapel. Mayhap, I thought, John Kellet had heard rumors which he might share with me. Not from the confessional, of course. His standards are higher than Father Harold's. Would the cleric share hearsay with me when folk of his tiny parish would not? There was but one way to discover this.

Kellet had not oiled the hinges to the chapel door for some time, so the squeal when I pushed the door open alerted him to a visitor. He called down from his chamber in the squat tower and a moment later I saw him descend the stairs.

"I give you good day," the priest said, and tugged a forelock. This he did not need to do. No priest ordained by Holy Mother Church need show obeisance to a gentleman, but I believe John Kellet cannot divorce himself from his common origin.

There was no reason to conceal with many words the reason for my visit. And John Kellet is a forthright man who appreciates candor. "I have come to hear the latest town gossip," I said. Then added, "I do not ask you to tell what men may have confessed."

"Not like that new priest, eh?"

The revelation shocked me. Father Harold's indiscretion had already traveled to St. Andrew's Chapel.

"You know of this?" I said. "Do others?"

"Can't say. I heard from Robert Baker."

"Why did he speak of it? What reason did he give?"

"Didn't, really. I went yesterday to purchase two loaves and we got to talkin'. Robert is one to enjoy a bit of chat, you know."

I nodded. He and Maud are well suited.

"Don't know why the subject come up. When it did Robert seemed remorseful. . . like he'd spoke out of turn, without thinkin'."

"He did. I ask you not to share this with any other man. The matter is being sorted out."

"Can't imagine Father Thomas nor Father Ralph would accept such a violation from that new priest."

"They will not. Nor Lord Gilbert, either."

"Then the man is not long for Bampton, eh?"

"So 'tis hoped. What other gossip have you heard recently? Do folk speak of widowers showing interest in Leuca Harkins? I saw a man talking to her a few minutes ago. A stranger to Bampton."

"Oh, that would be Ewen, Leuca's brother. He's worried about her, folk do say. Comes all the way from Curbridge, which ain't easy for 'im, what with 'is bad foot."

"From Curbridge? How often does he do so?"

"Don't know. Once or twice a week, I hear."

"A bad foot, you say?"

"Aye. Some Frenchman chopped off half 'is right foot with an axe at Poitiers."

"Poitiers? That battle was twenty years ago."

"Aye. Ewen's much older than Leuca. She be 'is little sister, so 'e looks out for her, folk do say."

"He must have been angry that Edmund mistreated her so," I said.

"Surely. But what could he do? Crippled like 'e is he'd not contend with Edmund. An' Ewen's a small man. Edmund outweighed 'im by two stone at least."

The man I'd seen speaking to Leuca was indeed small. Not much taller than Leuca, and slight of build. Whether or not he walked with a limp I could not tell, for he took no steps whilst I looked his way. Might he be the man who pierced Uctred at the Ladywell? Why would he do so? What had Uctred to do with Leuca or her family?

I had no answer to this question, but decided to return to Rosemary Lane and observe Leuca's brother. If that was the visitor I saw. There was a chance 'twas not.

I bade Father John good day and walked briskly to Rosemary Lane. Two of Leuca's children were playing in the toft, the older was plying a wooden spade, digging droppings from the hen house into the soil. Of Leuca or her male visitor there was no sign.

There was yet an hour 'til noon and my dinner. And if I was late for the meal, what matter? The best I could expect was stockfish. 'Twas a fast day. More than likely I would find a pottage set before me. This would be as tasty as Kate could make it, but there is only so much that can be done with peas or beans.

I set off on the road to Brize Norton and Curbridge. If Ewen walked with a limp I might soon catch him and observe his pace from a distance, unseen. Uctred had said his attacker walked with a slight limp, which had not slowed his escape much. Mayhap I should walk the road with a lively pace if I was to observe his stride and return to Galen House in decent time for my dinner.

I caught Leuca's brother just before reaching the place where the roads to Brize Norton and Curbridge diverge, barely more than a mile from Bampton. Having part of a foot lopped off must be a painful experience, but Ewen had learned to live with the handicap. His limp was barely discernible and slowed him only a little.

I had intended to travel the road to Curbridge until I could observe Ewen's stride, then return to Bampton. His gait certainly fit Uctred's description of his attacker's pace. But then I saw something which required closer examination.

The man walked purposefully, taking no heed of what might be behind him. I closed to within fifty or so paces of the fellow, from which proximity I could see a mended slash across the back of his brown cotehardie. His beard, which I had glimpsed as he stood in Leuca's toft, was beginning to grow gray. From behind I could not see the buttons which closed his cotehardie. Were they of bone? Was one missing?

I had seen what I needed to see, so stopped and watched Ewen disappear around a bend in the road. Never once had he looked over a shoulder to see if he was followed. Why would he? A poor man has little fear of being set upon and robbed on the road. What if I had coughed, or made some other sound to indicate my presence? Would I have learned anything from his reaction?

Leuca's brother had intended to slay Uctred. I was sure of this. But why? Uctred had said he did not know and had never before seen his attacker. What possible enmity could Ewen feel for a man he did not know? After dinner I must speak to Uctred of what I had learned. Mayhap he would recall meeting Leuca's brother some time in the past.

Kate and Adela had prepared stockfish in galyntine sauce. I was in time to enjoy the meal and avoid Kate's reproach for being tardy for a repast she had worked diligently to prepare. I was tempted to explain to her why I was nearly late for dinner but decided to wait for evening when Adela would be away. This was a favorable decision.

"You are eager to be away," Kate said.

I was gobbling my meal, saying little, thinking of what I must tell Uctred of my encounter with Leuca's brother. "There is a matter newly discovered which I must speak about to Uctred. I will tell you of it tonight. Mayhap it is of no importance."

"You would not be so hasty at your dinner if what you learned this morning was of no consequence."

My Kate knows me well.

I found Uctred alone, sitting in a chair rather than reclining in bed. Not a bench, a chair, with a padded cushion. He saw me appraising it and spoke. "Lord Gilbert called just before dinner. I was sittin' on me bed. He seen an' sent this chair."

"'Tis from the solar, I think," I said.

Uctred looked down at the chair and seemed to rise from it, as if the piece was too grand for the rump of a mere groom.

"You 'ere to see if I'm gettin' better?"

"Aye. That and another matter."

"Still some blood when I pass water. Not so much, I think. When'll I be able to leave me sickbed an' live normal, like?"

"Not for another week, at least. Are you bored with this chamber?"

"Aye. Gettin' so I'd rather muck out the stables than spend another day 'ere."

"You must be feeling better," I smiled. "Now, about that other matter. Have you ever known a man from Curbridge?"

"Curbridge? Nay. Passed through there once or twice, I think. Once with you an' Arthur, as I remember."

"So far as you know you've made no enemies from that village?"

"Nay. That where the man who pricked me is from?"

"So I believe."

"Why, an' you don't mind me askin'?"

I didn't, but at that moment Cicely returned to the guest chamber. Until I had a better notion as to why Leuca Harkins' brother would trouble himself to come from Curbridge to Bampton for the purpose of slaying Uctred I thought the fewer folk who knew of my suspicion the better. I tilted my head toward Cicely and did not reply.

Uctred is no dolt. He understood my silence and changed the subject. "So if in a week I'm passin' no blood, an' me ribs don't hurt much, I can get on with me duties?"

"Aye. For a man wounded as you were your recovery is splendid."

"An' you'll take them stitches out of me ribs then?"

"Probably. I mustn't be hasty, else the wound, small as it is, might reopen. You'd not want me to practice my needlework on you anew."

Cicely listened to this exchange, then spoke. "'E going to need lookin' after much longer?"

"Nay. Someone will need to bring his meals and empty the chamber pot. But you need not stay with him all day and night."

"Good. 'E's become sour as old verjuice."

I looked to Uctred and he cast down his eyes.

"Cicely," I said, "volunteered to care for you when you were brought here insensible and knocking at the gates of pearl. Have you now been treating her badly in return for her ministry?"

"Reckon I've been a little sharp," he said softly.

Cicely stood, hands on hips, and said, "A little? I've begun to wish the man who stabbed you 'adn't made a botch of it."

167

"If remaining in this chamber, with a soft bed for the night and now a cushioned chair for the day, is disagreeable to you I will tell Lord Gilbert you are recovered enough that you can do whatever you will which does not cause pain. Is that your wish?" I asked.

Uctred looked to the feather-stuffed mattress, considered his situation, and spoke. "Been takin' out me frustrations on any who 'appen to be near," he said. "Right sorry I am. Not accustomed to folk doin' for me. Usually it's me doin' for others."

Cicely's demeanor relaxed, the lines on her face softened. "This mean you'll not complain no more?"

"Aye," Uctred said. "Be as obedient as a lamb."

"Hah," Cicely replied. "I should live so long. I'll see to your supper," she continued. "'Til then you can do for yourself. I've other work to attend to." She departed the chamber and closed the door behind her. Firmly.

"Regarding Curbridge," I said. "This morning I followed a man from Bampton most of the way to Lew. He walked with a limp, his beard was turning to gray, and he wore a brown cotehardie."

"Many folk like that about," Uctred said.

"Aye. But has the back of their cotehardie been slashed, then mended?"

That question arrested Uctred's attention. "What was the fellow doin' in Bampton that you decided to follow when 'e left?"

"His name is Ewen. He is Leuca Harkins' brother. I saw him speaking to her in her toft and discovered from John Kellet who he was. Although I suppose others in Bampton know this as well. Leuca's friends, at least. Thought at first he was a suitor."

"Leuca's brother tried to slay me? What've I done to 'er would make 'im do so?" Uctred was genuinely puzzled. "An' I never seen 'im before. Whatever grudge 'e bears me I can't guess."

"'Twill have something to do with Edmund's death," I said.

"You think the fellow believes I murdered Edmund?"

"I don't know what to think, but I don't believe that would be the cause for his attack. For one thing, from whom would he hear such a fable? No one in Bampton has bandied such a rumor about. Not that I've heard."

"Me neither," Uctred agreed. "You going to speak to Leuca 'bout this? Why 'er brother would stick me?"

"Not yet. Not until I know more. If I did she would find a way to send word to Curbridge and Ewen would be away."

Chapter 12

Lord Gilbert demands to be informed of events in his manor, even down to the smallest details. Murder and an attempt to murder are not small details. When I left the guest chamber I sought John Chamberlain and asked to speak to my employer. He was, I learned, entertaining guests in the solar. Lord Gilbert is a popular host, and never wants for visitors. He is a hospitable man, and known for keeping an excellent table. Many gentlemen traveling with their ladies find it convenient to interrupt their journey at Bampton for a few days.

Lord Gilbert's guest this day was Sir Geoffrey Hallam, of a manor near to Chester. I do not remember his lady's name. She was not a beauty so as to imprint upon a man's mind. Likely her value to her husband lay not in her face but in her dowry.

I did not wish to discuss manor business with Sir Geoffrey and his wife listening. Whatever I said would be discussed as the couple and their retainers journeyed north, 'til much of the west country would know of mayhem in Bampton.

I had in the past desired to speak privily to Lord Gilbert of Bampton matters when he was with guests. He was adept at finding ways to suggest their departure. This day he advised the knight and his lady that they might wish to retire to their chamber to prepare for supper. He had used this ruse successfully in the past. A suggestion from Lord Gilbert, Third Baron Talbot, should be heard as a command.

Sir Geoffrey took the hint, suggested to his lady that they seek their chamber, and a moment later John closed the solar door behind them.

"That priest at St. Andrew's Chapel knows more of what happens in Bampton than any other man," Lord Gilbert said when I told him of Leuca and her brother. "If a thing is said or done in my manor ask Kellet about it, not me. How does he know so much, I wonder?"

"Keeps his lips mostly closed and his eyes and ears open," I replied.

"Hah. Like the holy man. Put the two together and there'd be no secrets in Bampton. Well, not many. You think Leuca's brother came here to slay Uctred because he believes Uctred murdered his brother-in-law?"

"Nay. Ewen would likely have hated Edmund for mistreating his sister and bear no ill will against the man who slew him."

"What, then? Did the man slay Edmund to free his sister from abuse? If so, why attack Uctred? Shall I send men to Curbridge to seize the fellow?"

"Not yet."

"We might rack the man to learn his role in Edmund's murder."

"We might. But men so tormented will say whatever they believe will end the pain. We might learn truth, we might not."

"Hmm. Mayhap."

Lord Gilbert was not convinced of my logic. If I failed to discover Edmund Harkins' killer he would recall that I had disparaged his recommendation. This would not augur well for my continued employment. The bone button continued to insert itself into my thoughts. It seemed that Ewen had attacked Uctred. If his cotehardie was closed with bone buttons and one of these was missing, the absence might put him at Edmund's forest grave. How could I gain a close inspection of Ewen's garment?

Curbridge is but three miles from Bampton, and I am known there. If I spent an hour or so prowling through the village, folk would take notice and remark to each other of the strange behavior of Bampton's bailiff. Was there some man new to Bampton who might pass through Curbridge watching for an inhabitant who wore a cotehardie missing a bone button?

Aye, there was. Janyn Wagge.

The day was growing late, and nights become long as November draws near. I told Lord Gilbert that I wished to send Janyn Wagge to Curbridge, and the reason for the visit. He agreed to spare the youth for a day, so I sought the lad before I departed the castle to tell him the rudiments of what I had planned for him.

When I found Janyn and told him that Lord Gilbert had assigned him to assist me Saturday morning the youth grinned broadly. I told him to meet me at Galen House at the second hour.

He was prompt. We set off for Curbridge and as we walked I explained the reason for this excursion.

"Have folk in the castle spoken of the man found dead in the forest?" I asked. "You had not arrived when he was discovered."

"The man what got ate by hogs?"

"Aye. Edmund Harkins. What do Lord Gilbert's retainers say?"

"Got 'is due, most say. Beat 'is wife somethin' cruel."

"We are going to Curbridge because the wife's brother, Ewen, lives there. 'Tis nearly certain he stabbed Uctred whilst Uctred was praying at the Ladywell."

"Why'd 'e do that?"

"No man knows. Well, Ewen knows. 'Tis my belief the attack has to do with Edmund Harkins' death, but what that may be I cannot deduce. Some time after Edmund's corpse was found I spent time examining the pit where he was buried and found nearby a bone button. When Uctred was attacked he managed to draw his dagger and slash at the villain. I found a trace of blood on Uctred's dagger. Yesterday I saw a man visiting Leuca Harkins and learned 'twas her brother. I followed him toward Curbridge and came close enough to see a mended gash across the back of his cotehardie. I could not see the front, nor the buttons which closed the garment."

"You think 'e might be missin' a bone button?"

"Aye. But I am known in Curbridge, so if I am seen there folk might guess why. Ewen would."

"What d'you want of me?"

"Ask in the village for Ewen. When you find him see does he have a button missing from his cotehardie. He will wonder who you are and why you seek him. Do not mention your name. Say that you bear a message from Leuca. She wishes to see him. When he arrives in Bampton Leuca will, of course, disavow the request, but you need some excuse for seeking Ewen. Word from Leuca will do as well as any, and if Ewen describes you to Leuca she'll not recognize you. You're known to folk of the castle, but not, I think, in the town. Not yet."

The road to Curbridge curves just south of the village. I waited there and sent Janyn to seek Ewen. What next occurred I did not see, but learned from Janyn.

The first person he saw upon entering the village was a woman who had just then gathered eggs from her hen house. She knew Ewen Lusk's house and directed Janyn to the hovel. The dwelling was in need of new thatching. Daub, Janyn said, had fallen from the walls in several places. 'Twas the house of a poor cotter. Likely why Uctred described Ewen's cotehardie as threadbare and tattered, and why the man's wife did what she could to mend it, rather than discard the garment.

Ewen's cotehardie, Janyn said, had no buttons at all, wood or bone. 'Twas of the old sort, loose enough to be drawn over a man's head. Did Ewen own another? Not likely, else he'd not don something which so advertised his poverty.

I was somewhat surprised by the discovery. I had persuaded myself that Ewen had slain Edmund, or was one of a band which had done so. That was yet a possibility, the bone button having been ripped from some other member of the murderous group. But Janyn's report did nothing to prove it so. I had good evidence that Ewen had attacked Uctred, but no proof the assault had anything to do with Edmund Harkins' death.

Janyn told me of his brief conversation with Ewen as we returned to Bampton. We turned from Broad Street to pass St. Beornwald's Church and travel thence to Galen House. As we did I glanced back and saw Ewen hurrying our way, his limping gait more conspicuous due to haste. Evidently Janyn's falsehood that Leuca wished to speak to him had put wings to Ewen's heels. I dislike deceiving folk, even in a good cause. But who knows? Mayhap Leuca did want to speak to Ewen. It's possible.

Ewen surely saw two men enter Bampton a few hundred paces ahead of him. Did he realize that one of these had delivered a message to him? Janyn's form is recognizable. If so, did he wonder who the messenger's companion was?

I told Janyn to join me in Galen House. From a ground floor window I watched Ewen hurry past and disappear into Rosemary Lane.

It would not do for Ewen to see Janyn, so I told the lad to leave Galen House through the kitchen door, cross the toft, then wade across Shill Brook near to the Ladywell. He would be at the castle in time for his dinner, which a youth of his age and size would not want to miss.

I was curious as to the reception Ewen would receive when he greeted Leuca. So after I sent Janyn on his way I followed Ewen, but not closely. When I reached Rosemary Lane I glanced in the direction of Leuca's house and saw her and Ewen in the toft. I was too far away to hear their words, but both gesticulated vigorously. I could imagine the conversation.

Did my instruction to Janyn that he was to tell Ewen of Leuca's wish to speak to him give brother and sister a hint that someone suspected Ewen to be a malefactor? And if so, was that bad? A man who believes his evil is found out, or nearly so, may behave in a suspect manner. In trying to draw attention away from himself he does the opposite. So I hoped.

I had enough evidence against Ewen to charge him before the King's Eyre with wounding Uctred, but yet thought his conduct might have to do with Edmund's slaying. If I watched his behavior from afar, would he gather enough planks to build his own scaffold?

As I was near I continued my journey to the castle. Was Uctred mended enough that his petulance had returned? Aye. He had promised to amend his conduct toward

Cicely, but when I entered the guest chamber I found him berating her for the ale she had brought. 'Twas gone stale, he complained, as if that was her responsibility.

When Uctred saw me pass through the doorway he fell silent, remembering, I believe, his promise to correct his behavior. He would not, I decided, 'til he was free of the guest chamber, which he had come to view as a gaol.

An empty trencher sat on a table beside his chair. I saw a few crumbs and stockfish bones upon it, the remains of an early dinner.

"Your appetite has returned?" I asked.

"Aye," he said. Sheepishly.

"And your bellyache? Does it return after you've eaten well?"

"Nay. Well, not much."

"Stand, then bend and touch your toes as close to the flags as you can."

Uctred did so. He winced, but managed to touch his ankles, which would be an achievement for a man of his age even had he not had a dagger plunged into his side.

"You need no longer remain a convalescent," I said. "I will tell Lord Gilbert you are well enough to resume light duties. But you must listen to your gut. If you do a thing which causes pain, stop at once. I will not yet remove the stitches, not for another week."

Uctred brightened at this. The guest chamber, for all its amenities, no longer appealed. He desired to be with his friends, doing as he had always done. Perhaps this was the best physic I could prescribe.

My dinner would soon be ready, so I hurried to the solar to tell Lord Gilbert of Uctred's remarkable recovery.

"I will assign him to the marshalsea," Lord Gilbert said, "and tell Sir William to set him to light work for a week or so. . . currying the horses and oiling harnesses would serve, I think."

I agreed and set off for home. I did not soon arrive there, for as I passed under the portcullis I saw three dusty horsemen enter the forecourt. 'Twas Sir Jaket, Thomas, and Richard who rode toward the drawbridge. They had traveled to Exeter and returned in a week! They would have changed mounts along the way, but their beasts would require Uctred's attention. And the riders would be saddle sore and have no desire to mount a horse for a few days.

Sir Jaket swung stiffly down from his ambler and I greeted him as he pounded dust from his tunic. "Have you a reply to Lord Gilbert's letter?"

"Aye." The knight opened a saddlebag and withdrew a sheet of parchment, folded and sealed. "Where is Lord Gilbert?" he said. "In the solar?"

"Aye. Awaiting dinner. He will be eager to read the bishop's reply."

Sir Jaket set off for the outside steps to the solar, with myself, Thomas, and Richard close behind. I was probably more interested than Lord Gilbert in the contents of the letter. The bishop's decision would affect both me and Adela.

Sir Jaket banged upon the solar door and I heard John Chamberlain say, "Enter."

Sir Jaket did so, with me at his shoulder, and held the folded parchment before him.

Lord Gilbert grinned, took the letter, broke the seal, then frowned. Had he scanned the message so quickly? Was it a denial of his request? Neither of these.

"Hah. 'Tis writ in Latin," he barked, then looked to me.

I was the only man in the solar who knew Latin well. Lord Gilbert knew this, handed me the letter and said, "What does the old reprobate say?"

I wrote of the message several days later, so do not remember a verbatim account, but in general the bishop granted Lord Gilbert's request. Bishop Brantyngham told his nephew that the press of duties required that he seek a trusted aide. The bishop wrote that he could think of no man more capable of shouldering the responsibility than Father Harold, and that in a few days he would send an archdeacon and servants with a cart to return his possessions and himself to Exeter.

The bishop had been careful to obscure the real reason for Father Harold's removal. He ended the letter by writing that, as one of Lord Gilbert's retainers was at that time present in Exeter, he would dispatch the letter to Lord Gilbert and ask him to send it on to Father Harold.

Lord Gilbert smiled as I read the missive. As did I. All we'd hoped was achieved. Nothing in the letter spoke of a replacement for Father Harold, but this did not trouble me. Whomever the bishop chose he could hardly be more troublesome than his nephew.

Would Father Harold, in the few days remaining to him in Bampton, redouble his designs against Adela, or even demand that she accompany him to Exeter? What new threat could he deliver?

Lord Gilbert instructed John Chamberlain to bear the letter to Father Harold. I excused myself and hurried to Galen House. For two reasons. I was hungry and 'twas time for dinner. And I had thought of a way to protect Adela for a few days.

As I trotted past Rosemary Lane I glanced toward

Leuca's house. Neither she nor her brother was visible. What conversation had I missed?

Dinner this day was stockfish in balloc broth. I told Kate and Adela of Bishop Brantyngham recalling his nephew, then tactfully – Bessie was listening – suggested that until Father Harold was away Adela might want to reside at Galen House. The ground floor room I use when treating patients was unused, and unless some man did something careless with an edged tool it was likely to remain so. The chamber was equipped with a pallet for those occasions when an affliction required a man to recline. So long as Adela was within Galen House Father Harold could trouble her no more. Probably.

The lass was cheered at this news and readily accepted the offer to remain at Galen House. I told her that when Christopher called to accompany her to the Weald I would tell him of the temporary change, and also that he must inform her father that no new threat against him or Adela should be considered, as Father Harold was summoned to Exeter, where he would no longer vex the family.

When Christopher heard the news later he was as crestfallen as Adela was pleased. The clerk had enjoyed his duty. It is always good when a man finds an obligation also a delight. Well, almost always.

Ewen Lusk had probably returned to Curbridge, where he would go about his business unaware, I thought, that I knew of his attempt on Uctred's life. I intended to be careful in the next few days that I did not cause him to suspect I knew of his malfeasance. Should he take a notion that I guessed of his attack at the Ladywell he might pack up wife, family, and goods in a handcart and be off to some distant manor whose lord would offer rent low enough to attract an absconding tenant, ignoring the Statute of

Laborers. 'Tis an easy matter these days for a man to change his place if he is of a mind to do so. 'Tis a wonder more men do not.

Did Uctred plan to renew his visits to the Ladywell, beseeching St. Frideswide to renew his sight? I had not asked. If he did, I would advise he take a companion with him. Ewen Lusk might know his wound had not been fatal, so make another attempt. But why had he done so in the first place, and how did he know Uctred could often be found at the Ladywell? If I could not discover the answers to these questions in the next few days I would apprehend Ewen and get the explanation from his lips. If he refused to account for his motive I could mention Lord Gilbert's suggestion. The thought of the rack might loosen his tongue.

I stopped at the bridge whilst on my way to the castle and stared into Shill Brook's pellucid flow. My dunking in the stream returned to my mind. Was Uctred attacked for the same reason I was tossed into Shill Brook? If so, mayhap I am fortunate that I returned home only cold and wet, unpierced.

"Leave it be," the voice had said. I had not obeyed. Did those who plunged me into the brook have some worse indignity in mind if I continued to search for Edmund Harkins' slayer?

Why? The man had few friends. Were his foes so pleased with his death they would attack any man who approached near the truth of his demise? Numbering those of Bampton who disliked Edmund was a more difficult task than tallying those who liked him. For the latter group I had enough fingers to count on, but not for the former.

At the castle I walked to the marshalsea, where Lord Gilbert said Uctred would be assigned. He was there, currying one of Lord Gilbert's favorite dexters. I recognized the beast as an irritable animal given to kicking and biting the unwary, but, Lord Gilbert claimed, courageous in the heat of battle. The horse stood quietly under Uctred's ministrations. Uctred spoke soothing words to the beast as he worked the currycomb and in response the animal flicked ears and tail.

Uctred saw my shadow darken the stable door and turned to see who interrupted his labor. "Don't step too close," he said. "Trajan don't like folks comin' up behind 'im. He'll plant a hoof in yer ribs."

"Does work with the horses agree with you?" I asked.

"Oh, aye. Seems to me I tire sooner than I did, though."

"That is to be expected. You suffered a grievous wound. Do you plan to visit the Ladywell again?"

"Aye. If the water an' the saint can't restore me sight, figure nothin' else will."

"You should not go there alone."

"What? You think the man what did for me might strike again?"

"You do not know why he did so, nor do I, but whatever the reason it likely yet exists. If he wanted to slay you a few days past he probably still does. Arthur's son, Janyn, is a sturdy lad. One look at him and a man with wicked intent will reconsider his purpose."

"Aye, an' I'll 'ave me 'and close to me dagger while I beseech the saint."

"A wise plan. Holy Writ says a man is not to repay evil with evil, nor resist a wicked man, but it also says men must not commit murder. It must not be a sin to prevent another from doing a sin. Especially a sin which cannot be undone."

"'Twould ease my mind some," Uctred said, "if I could reckon what I done to cause a man to stick me."

"You've thought much on this?"

"Near every hour of every day, an' yet nothin' comes to me. An' another thing. . . when I was out amongst folk in town, men would have naught to say to me. Others, of the castle, wasn't offish, but townsfolk would turn their backs if they seen me comin'. Not as if I had cause to venture to the town much, but when I did I got the cold shoulder."

"This was before you were attacked? Well, of course. You've had no opportunity to visit the town since you were stabbed."

"Nay, an' don't wish to."

The sun was low in the west, or would be were it not obscured by clouds, and time for supper drew near. I left Uctred to his occupation, departed the castle, and met a man I would have preferred to avoid where the lane to the Weald joins Mill Street. Father Harold was departing the Weald, red-faced. If he were a kettle he'd have been steaming. Where in the Weald had he been?

"You will regret your impertinence," he growled.

"Impertinent? Me? Nay, I am a model of civility. Especially where helpless maids are concerned."

"My uncle will learn of your heresies."

"Heresies? Am I guilty of more than one? Will you name them so I may amend my ways?"

"You deny the teaching of Holy Mother Church."

"Hmm. Which is most foul, I wonder: to do a thing Holy Writ condemns – fornication, for example – or to believe a thing Holy Church condemns?"

'Twas unfortunate that we traveled in the same direction, I to Galen House, he to continue past to his vicarage. We exchanged unpleasantries as we strode Church View Street. These I will not relate, as we are told to be kind to those who despitefully use us. This is a difficult command, which I did not at the time succeed in obeying.

What Father Harold's business in the Weald was did not enter our conversation. I thought I could guess. A few hours earlier he had read his uncle's letter. I suspected he had gone to Stephen Parkin's house for a last attempt at coercing Adela to come away with him. Not finding her at home he had probably resorted to one last threat against her father. If Parkin had replied as I advised 'twould account for the priest's petulance. What accounts for his petulance on other days I cannot guess.

The walk homeward had left me in a foul mood. This, however, did not last long. Adela was as cheerful as I had seen her in many days. She saw, I think, an end to her plight. My Kate's nausea had vanished, her appetite returned, and she was joyful that we would soon add to our brood. Bessie finds pleasure in each new day. Ah, to be a child again. And John understood that 'twas nearly time for supper. This was enough to make him gladsome. My ennui soon dissipated, surrounded as I was with blythe spirits, and I forgot Father Harold's unpleasant company.

I even managed, for a time, to forget that I had a murder to solve. Sunday morning dawned bright and fair, the weather leading to felicitous thoughts into which even death and duty found it difficult to intrude. The bell in St. Beornwald's tower rang for mass, and Galen House emptied as we joined the flow of worshipers on Church View Street.

Some parish residents greeted us as we joined the procession but many marched resolutely on and did not acknowledge me or Kate in any way. A few of those who ignored me nodded almost imperceptibly to Adela. Many of these were residents of the Weald.

The rota for the homily that day fell to Father Harold. Or so it appeared. But mayhap he had requested of Father Thomas and Father Ralph that he be allowed to address the parish a last time before he departed Bampton.

His remarks were not complimentary. His criticism of the parish did not extend to Lord Gilbert. He was more careful than to castigate a baron of the realm who had the power to make his life miserable beyond what his uncle could deflect. The others of us were a helpless target of his wrath. We were all sinners – well, he was correct on that point – doomed to perdition unless we amended our ways. That was surely true for some portion of his congregation.

Father Thomas and Father Ralph squirmed during this denunciation. Fortunately the vitriol did not last long. Father Harold exhausted his vocabulary of censorious terminology, turned from the nave, then sat scowling over the congregation. 'Twas left to Father Thomas to conclude the mass and send the pax board through the worshipers. I cannot speak for others, but when the pax board came to me I felt more like taking a bite from it than kissing it.

Folk were discussing Father Harold's accusations as they departed the churchyard. They exchanged whispered comments behind raised hands, as if fearful the angry priest, even though he would soon depart, might hear and afflict them for their views.

As we passed under the lychgate some words from Father Harold's homily which had passed unnoticed in the hurricane of his denunciations came back to me. "The felons among you are known," he had roared, "and will suffer the penalty due unless indemnity follows confession."

What indemnity? Penance follows confession. But indemnity? What does that follow? What did he mean?

And who knew of felons? Not me, try as I might. Were these words a reference to the violation of the confessional of which Father Harold stood accused? Were those who confessed to slaying Edmund Harkins assigned today a fee for Father Harold's silence? This seemed far-fetched, but what else could his words, so openly uttered, have meant? Surely this day I'd heard a threat, and as he would in a few days leave Bampton 'twould soon be carried out. One way or another.

"You are silent," Kate said as we approached Galen House. "Are you considering Father Harold's tirade? He was most vengeful."

"He was that. But he will soon be away and we will no longer trouble ourselves with his enmity."

"What trouble may his rancor cause in the days he remains?" Kate asked.

"Who can know? James the apostle said the tongue is a terrible scourge. Father Harold's wanton tongue could do the town much harm. Many years might pass to undo the mischief done by a few careless words."

"Mayhap they are not careless, but intended," Kate said.

"Aye. That also."

Dinner this day was froise and cryspes. I observed Adela as she prepared the meal and noted that the light-hearted conduct she had exhibited Saturday was gone. She went about her duties silently, somberly. Mayhap Father Harold's homily had deflated her. Why so? She was soon to be free of his unwanted attention. She was no felon from whom an indemnity was demanded. Was she?

Chapter 13

The rest of the day was cloudy, which added to the gloom with which Father Harold's homily had begun the morning. As night came I went to bar the door and through a window my eye caught movement in the street. Who, I wondered, would be about after curfew? He had best hurry to be home before John accosted him. Mayhap 'twas the holy man.

I moved closer to the window and saw a black-robed figure striding along Church View Street. A priest or clerk of St. Beornwald's Church. In his hand he carried a barely visible pouch. Father Harold's words came to me. I decided to follow the hurrying form to see which vicarage was his goal.

'Twas dark, and I was behind the man, but when he entered Father Harold's vicarage I knew who it must be. Randall, his clerk, was tall and lean, as was this man. Where had he gone so late of a Sunday evening, and for what purpose?

An errand for Father Harold, no doubt. Could I pry from him what nocturnal assignment had been given him? Would he know of Father Harold's dislike for my views – or what the priest believed my views are? If I could find him alone would he answer questions about his duties? Not unless some threat was held over him which he would consider a greater menace than Father Harold's ill will.

Rain fell heavily upon the tiles of Galen House roof in the night and woke me well before dawn. I lay abed and thought of Randall's evening appearance on Church View Street. With a pouch. What might a priest carry in a pouch? The host, mayhap, when visiting a dying parishioner. But Randall would accompany Father Harold for such duty and carry also a bell. Did Randall take something from Father Harold to some other man in the pouch, or was it the reverse? And was this man a resident of Bampton or the Weald? Why did I need to know? Because Lord Gilbert hired me to know what happens within his manor. And to inform him of what I learn.

I fell back to sleep, but some time later awoke again. 'Twas not the rain which this time disturbed my slumber. The torrent had become a drizzle, silently soaking the town. Kate shifted in her sleep and threw out an arm. Was her restlessness the cause of my wakefulness? Mayhap.

I once again sought Morpheus but he was not to be found. Had he crept into Galen House I would not have lain awake to hear the bar which secured the front door slide quietly into place.

The sound meant that the bar had earlier been lifted. Was this what woke me? Who would have crept from Galen House in the night? Not John. The lad could barely reach the bar standing on tiptoe. Bessie? I lifted the blanket, crept from our bed to the room where Bessie slept. I heard the child's regular breathing. I called her name softly. She did not stir, nor did her breathing change.

Adela, then, had flirted with danger and departed Galen House in the night. Where had she gone? And why? Had her time with Christopher caused her to seek the lad in the night for a tryst? I would confront her in the morning, after I'd sought the holy man. Perhaps he had seen her.

The rain had become a mist drifting from low clouds when I descended the stairs from our chamber. I had dressed myself quietly so as not to wake Kate. She usually left our bed before me, but not since announcing the pending increase to our family.

Adela was from her bed, had stoked the kitchen fire, and when she heard my feet on the stairs proceeded to spread parsley butter upon half a maslin loaf, with which I broke my fast.

Mayhap, I thought, Randall had visited Stephen Parkin last evening with some new threat from Father Harold. How a pouch could figure in some new demand I could not guess. But if I called upon Adela's father I would not need to guess. If 'twas he Randall visited Stephen would, I felt sure, answer honestly. I had earned his trust. So I thought. I said nothing to Adela about her nocturnal perambulation. Not yet.

Bampton's streets are either mud or dust. I cannot decide which I dislike most. My opinion doesn't matter. This day the Lord Christ decreed I would walk to the Weald through mud.

'Twas not a day for work in the fields. As I approached Stephen Parkin's hut I saw wisps of smoke trail from the gable vents before dissolving in the mist. Parkin was likely keeping warm and dry before his hearthstone whilst Adela's mother, Emmaline, set a kettle of pottage to simmer for the family dinner.

Stephen opened his crude door, which sagged alarmingly upon brittle leather hinges. He tugged a forelock when he saw who was at his door and asked how he might serve me.

"Mayhap I will serve you," I said. "Last evening, soon after dark, did you have a caller?"

"After dark?" he replied, as if he had not heard. He stood an arm's length away. Not far enough. His unwashed stench caused me to back away.

"A half-hour after curfew; no more," I said.

"Nay."

"Did you see any man on the path before your door?"

"Nay. Door was closed an' barred. Folk on the street that time o' night are usually up to no good."

The few windows of Parkin's hut were of oiled skin and opaque. No man could identify another through such a window.

"Indeed. Did you hear any man pass by about that time?"

"Nay. Told you, door was closed an' barred."

"I did not ask if you saw a man pass. Even through a closed door you might hear footsteps."

"Didn't, did I. Rain was heavy."

This was so, but hours after I saw Randall walk past Galen House.

During this conversation Adela's mother left her pot and came to stand behind her husband. Her cotehardie was threadbare and stained. Her hair was lank and tangled, unfamiliar with a comb. Was this how Adela would appear twenty years hence? Likely. Time is a thief no man – nor woman – can apprehend. Although most try.

I was taken aback by Parkin's attitude. In previous conversations he had been solicitous for my good will. This morning he was aloof. I had the opinion that even had he seen a man upon the path through the Weald, and the visitor had come to his door, he would not tell me of it. Why not?

I hoped the archdeacon and his retinue would arrive this day. Unless the archdeacon had previously visited

Bampton he would not know where to find Father Harold and would call at the castle for instruction. Would he arrive so early in the morning? Probably not. Likely he would have spent the night at some abbey, in which case he would reach Bampton no sooner than noon, as there are few monastic houses close by Bampton. The grange at Great Coxwell is nearest.

I could visit the castle to learn how Uctred fared. This would provide a good excuse if John Chamberlain or Sir William wondered why I lingered rather than being about my duties, although a bailiff does not need to explain himself to a chamberlain, or even a marshal. Did I feel guilty for sending Father Harold from Bampton? Nay. I might have accumulated numerous reasons for feeling guilty for one matter or another, but removing the deceitful priest was not one of them.

I found Uctred leaning upon a rake, exchanging castle gossip with Janyn. He and the lad had been put to work mucking out. I feared such labor might delay his recovery but he assured me that if he felt pain he would, as I instructed, cease the activity which brought discomfort.

There was no good reason to stay longer at the castle. Folk there were about their business and needed no advice from me as to how they might best complete it. I left the forecourt and turned to Mill Street, where I saw the holy man approach. He saw me at the same time, waved, and hurried his pace. We met near the bridge. I had intended to seek him and ask of Adela, so he was well met.

He beckoned me to follow, then set off past the castle. On the path leading to his hut he left the road. Trees and shrubs were now nearly bare of leaves and I saw his dwelling while still thirty or so paces from it. The holy man made no sign that he had something to tell me, but

I knew he must, else he would not have motioned me to attend him.

The mist had stopped. The forest air was still, so no draft passed through the gable vents of the hut. Smoke from the holy man's hearthstone fogged the interior. This did not seem to trouble the fellow, but I coughed violently and told him what he wished to tell me must be done outside. The holy man nodded and followed me out to fresh air.

Even with a tongue torn from his mouth it seems to me a man can make himself understood if he wishes. Of course, I've never tried to speak without a tongue so should be more charitable. Learning what the holy man wanted to relate would likely be a long process. Questions must be phrased which could be answered with a nod or shake of the head. I had two hours 'til dinner. What the holy man wanted to disclose took most of that time.

As was his practice, which I allowed for the information he often provided, the holy man had been about Bampton and the Weald well after curfew Sunday evening until rain drove him to his hut. He was not the only man creeping from shadow to shadow.

He had followed a black-clad figure to four houses. I asked him to show me where the man had gone. We left the wood, passed the castle, and turned to the path to the Weald. At Stephen Parkin's house the holy man nodded toward the dwelling, then walked on. Three doors past Parkin's hut the holy man stopped and pointed to a house. 'Twas the dwelling of Rolf and Beatrice Toty.

I asked if the black-clad figure had been received at both houses, and the holy man nodded, then turned to retrace his steps At Bridge Street he turned east and stopped where Rosemary Lane meet the High Street. Four houses line Rosemary Lane. The holy man pointed toward the narrow lane and I guessed which house had received a nocturnal visitor.

"Leuca Harkins?" I said. He nodded, then walked on. From the High Street we entered Catte Street. Peg Tyrrell was busy in her toft and curtsied as we passed. Godwin was at work with sticks and vines mending the hen house. When we were past the house the holy man tugged my elbow, glanced behind, and nodded toward the Tyrrells.

"Is that the other house visited in the night?" I whispered.

He nodded.

Priests and clerks wear black robes, but of course others may do so too if they wish to violate curfew and blend with the night. I had already seen Randall Creten on the streets near to dark. Did Randall leave Father Harold's vicarage then visit two families of the Weald and two of Bampton town? Who else? But how to know of a certainty, and how to discover why he did so?

We circled the town and at Galen House I invited the holy man to take dinner with us. He shook his head and walked on, content with his own pottage. So I thought.

The scent of a roasting capon greeted me. If any aroma could make a soul gladsome a fat capon dripping its juices to the embers should do it. But Adela greeted me with a doleful expression. For a day she had exhibited a pleasing countenance, and I thought I knew why. But only for a day. Other than Father Harold's homily I knew of no reason for the return of her mournful demeanor. The sermon had been villainous, to be sure, but most who heard it did not allow the words to dismay them so. It seemed to me Father Harold had caused more anger than distress among Bampton folk.

Was there some other reason for Adela's dejected appearance? If so, I could not guess its cause. Did her melancholy have to do with something she did or saw when she stole from Galen House in the night? Would the holy man know? He had not indicated that he had more to tell me of prowlers in the night. Mayhap he had reason for not doing so, if such was the case.

Bessie's doll was the main topic of conversation during the meal. Her grandfather had made it for her when she was a wee lass, and it had been handled and cuddled for many years. Now it needed repair, and I promised that I would see to it. Kate's father died when Bessie was but three years old, but my daughter claims to remember him well. The doll is the only object which can call forth his memory. I resolved to make it as nearly like new as I could. Mayhap some day Bessie's daughter will play with it and remember the codger who mended it. Will I some day become a codger? I suppose the alternative is to greet the Lord Christ beyond the gates of pearl. Perhaps a few years as patriarch will be acceptable.

Other than suspicions, which bailiffs are inclined to accumulate, I had no reason to suspect Adela might have crept away from Galen House in the night, or that the holy man had seen her. Did I really hear the bar slipping into place? A man might imagine strange things on a dark night. Should I challenge the lass or the holy man? Both? Or neither?

After dinner I set off for the holy man's hut. He had declined a meal at Galen House, which he would know, as 'twas not a fast day, would surely include flesh or eggs. Why would he choose a meal of pottage over pork or fowl? Folk do occasionally give the fellow a slab of bacon with which to flavor his pottage, or an egg or two when he lays hands upon their children and prays for their well-being. But if he had dined at my table any of these could be saved for another day.

The holy man was bent over his hearthstone, stirring a kettle of pease pottage when I arrived at his hut. A breeze had helped clear the fumes so a man might enter and not swoon for the smoke. The pottage was thick and green but I saw no pork as he stirred.

The door to the hut was open. When I entered, my shadow darkened the doorway, causing the holy man to look up. He saw who had entered, and went back to stirring his dinner, which seemed to me ready to consume.

The holy man never begins a conversation. He motioned me to sit on his bench, removed the bubbling pot from the hearthstone with a scrap of discarded wool to protect his fingers – the cast-off pot had no bail – then set the meal aside to cool.

When these tasks were accomplished he sat at the opposite end of the bench, stared at me, and waited for me to state my business.

Should I ask of what I did not know but suspected, or should I proclaim knowledge I did not actually have, hoping the holy man would assume I possessed wisdom I did not? Which would be most productive of truth? Assuming the holy man had withheld some information.

"You saw someone else upon Bampton's streets last night after curfew, did you not?"

The holy man stared wide-eyed at me, startled by the implication. He did not immediately reply, which was itself a reply. I believe he considered what harm he might do to himself if he answered truthfully. Or what trouble he might bring down upon himself if he answered falsely and I could prove it so. He finally nodded. Nearly imperceptibly.

If a man who could not speak could whisper, the holy man did so.

"You followed Adela Parkin?"

Another nod.

"She went to her home in the Weald?"

Again a nod.

"Did she go any other place?"

The holy man shook his head, then looked to his cooling pottage.

"Did Adela stay long at her parents' house?"

Another shake of his head.

"When she left she returned straightaway to Galen House?"

He nodded.

Something Adela learned during a brief visit to her parents in the middle of the night had brought gloom to settle upon her shoulders. Why did she go there? Did she expect to learn something? Was what she learned unexpected? The lass would tell me, I thought, rather than lose her position.

I left the holy man staring at his cooling pottage. Had my questions caused him to lose his appetite? Perhaps Adela could tell me why.

A flash of white appeared through the bare branches of the forest as I walked the path from the holy man's hut to the road. 'Twas the archdeacon. He rode a mule to indicate his humility. A man who must proclaim humility is generally not, and fears folk will not know of his modesty if he does not announce it in some manner.

Two riders, also mounted upon mules, and a man upon a cart drawn by another mule accompanied the archdeacon. I expected the entourage to approach the castle and was not disappointed. The man with the cart remained in the forecourt whilst the archdeacon and the other riders clattered across the drawbridge and disappeared through the gatehouse.

'Twas too late for dinner at the castle and too early for supper. I suspect the archdeacon expected to be invited to supper, due to his rank, but Lord Gilbert is unimpressed by most men's station, being one of the barons of the realm and able to look down on other men if he chooses to do so. And he often does.

I hurried to Galen House, not pausing at the bridge over Shill Brook. I would gaze into the stream some other time.

I found Adela in the toft, where she had just finished spreading linens to dry upon the bare branches of shrubs which lined the rear of my property. The pot in which the garments had been washed remained upon the cooling ashes. Filled with water the vessel was too heavy for Kate or Adela. 'Twas my contribution to wash day to bring out the pot, fill it, and when its use was done empty and store it 'til next wash day.

Adela glanced over her shoulder when I passed through the kitchen door into the toft. She turned back to her work, careful that none of the clean garments dragged in the mud. She expected me to tilt the pot and empty it, which I would do normally. But these were not normal days. When she finished stretching the last kirtle to dry she turned and found me standing before her, hands on hips, looking stern. I do not do stern very well. If I weighed two stone more, with a bull-like neck, my fiercest glare might cause fright among malefactors. Adela was no malefactor, so she seemed suitably impressed by my stormy stance and frown. She raised a hand to her mouth. She knew something was amiss, and swallowed like a fish tossed upon a riverbank.

"I granted you safety at Galen House," I began, "'til Father Harold was away. You repaid me by sneaking out last night to visit your parents. What was so important that you had to deal with the matter in the dead of night, without consulting me?"

She did not ask how I knew of her nocturnal visit home. She likely knew I learned of it from the holy man. Did she believe he would keep her curfew violation secret, I asked her?

"He promised to tell no man," she said softly.

"Not even me? Why would he do so?"

She did not reply for a moment. "I kissed him," she finally said.

"What?" I said. This was incredible to me.

"When I saw the holy man follow me home I begged him to keep silence and told him I would grant him a kiss if he swore to tell no man."

"You volunteered the kiss? He did not demand it as the price of keeping your secret?"

"Nay, sir. 'Twas my offer."

"Which he accepted?"

"Aye, sir," she blushed. "He did."

I wondered if the holy man had ever before received a kiss. He had not taken holy orders – so far as anyone in Bampton knew – so there was no stricture compelling him to abstain if a pert lass offered her lips. He would require a backbone of stone and a heart of ice to resist.

"He did not keep his vow," Adela finally said.

"Nay. But 'tis for your own good. What was so important that you needed to consult your parents in the middle of the night? Could the matter not wait 'til day? I asked you already. I require an answer."

"I told my father he must not pay," she said softly.

"Pay who? For what?"

"Randall."

"Father Harold's clerk demanded coins of your father?"

"Aye."

"What threat could the priest hold over your father that would cause him to give money to Randall?"

Adela did not reply but rather looked to the ground at her feet, as if she had seen some fascinating object there.

Whatever hold Father Harold had over Stephen Parkin it could not be a demand for Adela's service. She was safe in Galen House until the priest was away. Had Parkin been involved in some malfeasance about which Father Harold knew? Was this the subject of the confession which Maud Baker knew of? Mayhap the priest was enriching himself before departing Bampton by holding over men's heads information they would not want their neighbors or lord to know. Did this include Rolf and Beatrice Toty, Leuca, and Godwin and Peg Tyrrell? Was this the indemnity of Father Harold's sermon?

"If you will not speak, mayhap your father will," I said.

"Please do not trouble him," she cried.

"How else am I to learn why you advised him he must not pay Randall if you will not speak of it?"

"'Tis a private matter."

"No longer. I know of it. Some of it, at least. Are other folk involved in this private matter? Totys? Tyrrells? Leuca Harkins?"

Adela grew pale and chewed upon her lip.

"Did your father heed your advice?"

"Nay," she whispered. "I was too late."

Stephen Parkin was not at home. Emmaline said he was assisting Rolf Toty in planting a strip to rye. Here were two birds to kill with one stone.

I found the two men at work in a new-plowed field just beside the Aston road. Rolf strew seed from a sack hung from his shoulder and Stephen followed behind, dragging a crude harrow. The seed must be covered before voracious birds discovered and consumed it.

The two men walked the far end of the strip, so I waited at the road 'til they turned and approached. They seemed in no hurry to do so. When a lord's bailiff awaits them, most men, innocent or guilty, will seek reason to delay the meeting.

But the strip must be seeded and the soil raked over, so Stephen and Rolf finally came near and tugged forelocks when a few paces distant. They did not speak, assuming I would. They were correct.

"You were visited in the night, well past curfew," I began. "What was the caller's purpose?"

The men looked to each other and a silent message passed between them.

Rolf finally replied, "Nay. I'd no visitor last night. No man came to my door after curfew."

"Hmm. Before curfew, then? When 'twas dark but John was not yet upon his rounds?"

"Nay. Barred the door an' sought me bed when sun set."

I looked to Stephen. He anticipated the question and made a similar reply.

"You lie," I said. "Randall Creten was seen at your doors. Yours first," I said to Stephen, "then later at your house." I looked to Rolf.

"Who says so?" Stephen asked.

"Adela, your daughter, was also upon the streets last night. She told you not to pay Randall. Why would she do so? What debt did Father Harold seek to collect?"

"Adela did not tell you?"

"Nay."

"Then neither will I."

"Was it also a debt which the clerk wished to collect from you?" I said to Rolf. "If so, why seek payment in the night? What is the reason your neighbors should not know of Randall's mission, that he should appear in the night?"

Rolf evidently decided that recalcitrance might serve him equally as well as it did Stephen. He looked me in the eye but did not speak. 'Twas a dare to press the matter further.

What threat did I have to make either man speak? Raise their rents? I had no power to do so. They are the bishop's tenants. They need not obey me. They would surely prefer not to be on Lord Gilbert's bad side, but he is not their lord, the bishop is.

Stephen Parkin's daughter had told him that he should not give coins to Randall. Did Rolf or Godwin or Leuca give pence or groats to the clerk? If they did, was it to purchase Father Harold's silence in the matter of the confession he threatened to make known?

If the priest said nothing of the four families before he departed Bampton did this mean they had paid for his silence, the indemnity he required? Or was some other threat held over their heads of which I knew nothing and could but guess?

Rolf and Stephen stood silently, feet planted firmly, not shifting weight from one foot to the other as remorseful men might. I was defeated. They were not going to tell me why Father Harold's clerk visited them in the night, and no threat would make them do so. Could Leuca or Godwin be persuaded to speak? I am their bailiff and can exert leverage with them which cannot be applied to Rolf or Stephen.

I found Leuca at the same work Adela was about this day: washing the family kirtles and braes. Other wives and servants of the realm were likely at the same task, unless they had no aversion to filth and lice. Many do not.

Leuca looked up from stirring her pot, the contents of which for want of faggots was perhaps warm but not steaming. There was no reason to beat around the bush.

"How much did you pay Randall when he sought you last night? And why? What debt did you owe Father Harold?"

"Randall? Him what's Father 'arold's clerk?" She feigned ignorance. "Why'd 'e come 'ere in the night?"

"Precisely what I want to know. Do you claim he did not?"

"Aye."

"He was seen."

"Who says so? 'Twas that 'oly man what goes about in the night, meddlin' in other folks' business, weren't it?"

"You claim he lies?"

"Aye. Nothin' 'oly 'bout a liar."

"If so he is. I've found him truthful in the past."

"An' what of me? You think me dishonest?"

"Have you reason to be? The holy man has none."

"My Edmund was found near to 'is 'ut. Why so? You ever ask 'im?"

"Several times."

Leuca did not reply but returned to stirring her laundry. Like Rolf and Stephen she seemed to believe silence her best defense against my questions. But why did she need any such defense? Her husband's death was interwoven in this in some way, of this I was convinced. But how?

The wound over her left eye was now but a thin white line crossed at intervals by the marks of stitches. Should I mention the service I had provided her? Would she consider my work on her behalf to have created an obligation for her to cooperate? Apparently not.

"You believe 'im but not me?" she complained.

"I do. Although why you seek to deceive me is a puzzle. I intend to work it out. Yours is not the only house the clerk visited last night. He collected something – coins, I imagine – from you and three others, and carried it off in a pouch. What he gathered was for Father Harold, no doubt. There is a rumor about the town that the priest is betraying the confession of someone, or has threatened to do so. I wonder if the betrayal extends to folk of my bailiwick and he is requiring payment for his silence."

Leuca's face reddened but she would say no more. I heard slow hoofbeats and the creaking of cart wheels, turned, and saw the archdeacon and his servants pass by on Church View Street. Father Harold and Randall would be away tomorrow. Would trouble depart the town with them? Some, perhaps. And coins? Would the priest take silver with him to Exeter?

From Rosemary Lane I walked to Catte Street. Godwin Tyrrell was still at work on his hen house. His work was thorough. A fox that wished to enter would struggle to take a hen for its dinner.

Godwin saw me approach and ceased his labor. When I came near he tugged a forelock and greeted me pleasantly. Godwin has always been an affable fellow.

We are instructed to live at peace with all men and this injunction Godwin seems careful to follow.

"How may I serve you?" he said, rubbing the small of his back. Godwin has reached the age when performing stooped labor causes a man to stiffen.

"Last night, when all men should be behind closed doors, you received a visitor. What did Father Harold's clerk want?"

The calm smile which had greeted me vanished. I saw Godwin's fingers tighten about the vine he held until his knuckles became white. His round, pleasant face took on the appearance of a stone ogre I once saw upon Notre Dame de Paris.

Godwin cleared his throat, shuffled his feet, and appeared about to answer my question when Peg appeared in the door to their house. This is a substantial dwelling, of two bays. Godwin has nearly two yardlands of Lord Gilbert and hires poorer men at plow time and harvest.

Godwin looked to his wife and whatever he was preparing to say died on his lips. Had the woman heard my question? Possibly. Did she have an opinion about Godwin's reply? Most wives have opinions about what their husbands should do or say. If the husband is like Edmund Harkins the wife will likely hold her tongue. Godwin Tyrrell is not such a man.

Godwin and Peg were clothed alike, in cotehardies of russet wool. The garments were heavy and warm. Godwin's was thigh-length, and he wore gray chauces. Peg's cotehardie was ankle-length, as was the custom with women. Both were closed with bone buttons. I realized this with a start, and glanced to Godwin's cotehardie to see if a button was missing. None was.

Nor were any buttons absent from Peg's cotehardie, but I noticed an anomaly. Seven buttons closed the woman's garment. The upper six were dark with age and use, but the bottom button was pale, new.

Peg saw me studying the hem of her cotehardie, abruptly turned, and disappeared into the house. Godwin looked from me to the door and back again.

I found my tongue and asked again. "What was Randall Creten's purpose in visiting you last night?"

"Uh. . . Father Harold be soon away to Exeter. 'E sent Randall to, uh, say farewell an' offer a blessin'."

"Indeed? It was necessary to violate curfew to do this? He could not call upon you in the day?"

"Guess not. Busy man."

"Randall visited three other houses before he came here. Did he have the same duty there?"

"Mayhap. Didn't say."

"He carried a pouch, I'm told. What did it contain?"

"Saw no pouch."

"At one of the houses Randall visited, the occupant was told not to pay. The injunction was too late. Did you pay the clerk for Father Harold's good will? Or for some other debt? Some 'indemnity', the priest may have phrased it?"

"We owe naught to Father Harold, nor to any man, but our rent to Lord Gilbert."

"Who will be displeased to learn that Randall Creten was about after curfew last night and that you are concealing the reason he visited you."

Godwin and Peg had four children, all of whom had survived infancy – unlike most of their neighbors and Kate and me. The three oldest now peered out of the open door.

If I could not learn the truth of Randall's visit to Godwin and Peg from the father perhaps I might from the son. The oldest lad, Wilfred, was about ten years old. Old enough to be aware of events surrounding him, but mayhap not so old as to see a need to answer falsely a question the import of which he did not understand.

I turned from father to son and quickly strode the few paces to the lad.

"Wait," Godwin said, guessing my intent. I have been accused of being devious. Folk may be right.

"A man came to your house last night after curfew," I said to the lad. "What did your father give him?"

"Pennies," Wilfred said.

"What did the visitor say?"

"Much thanks."

"Was that all? Did he say more?"

"Said father was not to fret."

"How many pennies did your father give the man?"

The lad could not reply. Peg appeared, seized him by an ear, and the child howled as his mother yanked him into the house.

Godwin stood behind me, open-mouthed. I turned to him and asked the same question Peg had prevented his son from answering.

"How much did you give to Randall, and what did the coins buy?"

"Uh. . . Wilfred misspoke. He was abed, near asleep when the clerk called. No coins passed from me to Randall. The lad must have dreamed it. Aye, that's how it must've been. Wonderful imagination the lad has."

Peg reappeared at the door, shooing two younger children from the opening. I caught another glimpse of the lower button of her cotehardie as she did. There was no question but that it was a lighter hue than the others. I suppose the lowest button on a garment, especially a woman's cotehardie, is more susceptible to being torn free, and surely more likely to drag in the dirt and become discolored.

I was close enough to Peg that I could see the cotehardie buttons clearly. The upper, darker buttons were affixed with hempen thread through two button holes. The lower button had four holes through which the thread was passed. The button I found near to Edmund Harkins' grave had but two holes. Mayhap if such a button was ripped away, Peg decided to replace it with one more secure. Where did the original button vanish to?

The button I found at Edmund's grave was a dull white, colored with use and age. Much like six of the buttons on Peg's cotehardie. I had been seeking men who slew Edmund Harkins. Had I been on a fool's errand? Was it women who put the rogue in his grave? Could Leuca, Peg, Emmaline, and Beatrice have done so? Leuca and Emmaline are small women, but Peg and Beatrice are robust. If Godwin or Rolf struck his wife he might receive in return a blow which would convince him in the future to find some other way to express dissatisfaction with his spouse.

"If you will not tell me why Randall came to you in the night," I said to Godwin, "and why you gave him coins, I will seek Father Harold and discover from him what you will not disclose."

"Bah. He'll not speak to you."

"He may if Lord Gilbert demands he do so."

"His uncle be Bishop of Exeter. He'll not be in awe of Lord Gilbert."

"You know the priest is recalled to Exeter?"

"Aye."

"Do you know why?"

"Nay."

"Lord Gilbert requires it. Even a bishop will submit to a great baron's command. You think a village priest will not, no matter who his uncle may be?"

Godwin said nothing. It was clear that he, like Leuca, Rolf, and Stephen could tell me much but would not. Did they conspire together for silence? Surely. Did this reticence have to do with the confession Father Harold threatened to make known? And did that have to do with the death of Edmund Harkins? I thought the answer to all of these questions was "aye" but how to prove it?

Chapter 14

'Twas nearly time for my supper, and spending time at a trencher would be more welcome than trying to pry information from folk who wished me ignorant. It seemed their wishes were to come true.

Supper this night was arolettys. My frustration did not diminish my appetite. Few things do. I was pleased to see Kate consume a large portion of the custard. Adela, on the other hand, ate little. I thought I knew why. I thought wrong. Well, not completely wrong.

I intended to awaken early Tuesday morning, hoping to see Father Harold, the archdeacon, Randall, and the servants pass Galen House on their way to Exeter. I planned to smile at Father Harold as he passed. Godwin was probably right; confronting the priest would be fruitless.

I did awaken early, whilst the western horizon was yet dark, but not for the reason I had intended. I heard a rapping upon Galen House door, shouted to the visitor that I would attend him anon, then hastily drew on chauces and cotehardie.

'Twas John Whitestaff who stood before my door. The beadle doffed his cap and spoke. "Godwin an' Peg Tyrrell is gone," he said.

"Gone?" I said stupidly. Well, 'twas early morning.

"Aye. House is empty, door swingin' open. Goods gone. I seen a handcart behind the house last night on me rounds. Wondered about it. This mornin' I thought to pass the house an' see what use Godwin had for a handcart. 'Twas gone, an' them also."

'Twas Godwin Tyrrell who, with Uctred, was spreading manure from the castle marshalsea ten days past. From a handcart.

I did not wait for Father Harold and the archdeacon to pass. I hurried up the stairs, told Kate where I was bound, then set off with John for Catte Street.

'Twas as he said. The family was gone, the house empty of chattels but for beds, which were too bulky, even broken down, to transport on a handcart.

Since plague decimated the number of villeins and tenants 'tis not unusual for such folk to leave their manor in the middle of the night seeking lower rents and more agreeable masters. Illegal, but not unusual. But Godwin and Peg had not fled in the night with their brood for that reason. They knew something they did not want to tell me. Distance was the safest way to avoid me in the future. I followed the cart tracks to the High Street and saw them continue to the Aston road. Should I follow, or seek the castle and tell Lord Gilbert that a tenant had absconded?

Lord Gilbert must be informed. But not yet. Not 'til he had broken his fast. The news would anger him and the man bringing it would be most convenient to receive his wrath. So I returned to Galen House, consumed a maslin loaf and ale, then as dawn illuminated the spire of St. Beornwald's Church sought the castle to perform my dismal duty.

"Tyrrells?" Lord Gilbert said, one eyebrow raised. "They have near two yardlands, and they'll not find lesser rent for such land. And they abandoned a two-bay house. What were they thinking?"

"They did not leave Bampton seeking lower rents or better land or a greater house," I said.

"Oh? Why, then?"

"They know of a matter I seek to bring to light and wish to keep it dark."

"What can that be? What would they hide so important that they would abscond in the night?"

"It has to do with Father Harold betraying a confession, and that may have to do with Edmund Harkins' death."

"Ah. You think Godwin slew Edmund? And he knew you suspected him?"

"Nay. I believe Peg slew Edmund."

Lord Gilbert's eyebrow rose again. "What? A woman did the murder?"

"Not alone. I believe she had help."

"Can you prove this?"

"Nay, not yet."

"But you have a plan to do so?"

"Aye," I lied.

I stopped at Shill Brook to consider what I knew and what I did not know. The latter took more time than the former. The bridge is a good place to mull over things. I mull there often. As I watched the gentle current I remembered being pitched into the brook a few hundred paces south of the bridge.

Three men, their faces obscured, had tossed me into the stream at a place they had to know would not cause me to drown. 'Twas a message. "Leave it be," one had said – the same admonition which had been inscribed upon Galen House door.

Were my assailants Rolf, Godwin, and Stephen? I now suspected it so. And one of these had vanished. If four women slew Edmund Harkins, the husbands of three of these knew of the felony and sought to prevent their identification. What of Walter and Osbert? Edmund's plow team mates were choleric when they thought he had shirked his share of the labor. His death, however, did not cause them much grief even though they would now bear his portion of the work.

How did Leuca's brother and his attack on Uctred enter this muddle? Uctred is known in Bampton as being an occasional assistant of mine when investigating or apprehending malefactors. A few days before he was stabbed I spoke to him whilst he worked spreading manure. Godwin Tyrrell saw. Did he wonder what Uctred knew and what he might tell me? Was this suspicion relayed to Leuca, who in turn told her brother? They could not know what rumors Uctred might have heard, but were he dead what he did or did not know would make no difference.

Then why not slay me rather than simply heave me into Shill Brook? To slay a great lord's groom would be a serious crime, for which any lord would be furious. But to slay a lord's bailiff would be considered an even greater felony. And mayhap those who pitched me into the brook did not guess what Leuca's brother might do. Had they known, they might have cautioned against the attack.

My head was filled with suppositions. Some of which might be true. How to discover which? Godwin and Peg might be persuaded to tell me, if I could find them.

A handcart will leave a trail in mud and dust. Enough that I might follow the fleeing family? Surely the children, but for the babe, would walk. The cart would be full. Too full for riders, and heavy. Godwin could not keep up a rapid pace, nor could the children.

I finished mulling and sought Galen House and my dinner. Kate and Adela had prepared cormarye with wheaten loaves. As on Monday, Adela consumed little, Kate a hearty portion. I ate quickly, told Kate of my plan, then hurried to the castle to collect one of Lord Gilbert's palfreys. Adela neither spoke nor looked to me during the meal. Here was another matter to mull over.

As I crossed the drawbridge and entered the castle forecourt I saw Father Harold, the archdeacon, Randall, and the archdeacon's servants pass by on the road to Clanfield. They had not inconvenienced themselves to get an early start for Exeter.

Father Harold looked to the castle, saw me looking toward him, and scowled. He scowls quite well. Much practice, I assume. I lifted a hand and produced my broadest smile. He turned abruptly away and glared at the road before him as if it had offended him.

I collected a palfrey from the castle marshalsea, spurred the beast to a trot, and was soon past Aston. There had been little traffic, roads being unsafe, so the cart wheels were visible to Eynsham. But beyond Eynsham more folk found reason to travel toward Oxford and the wheel tracks became more difficult to follow, and eventually impossible.

I reined the palfrey to a halt while yet three or four miles from Oxford. If I did not immediately turn back I would not reach Bampton 'til dark. A thing I did not want to do.

And what if I found Godwin and Peg and demanded they return? Would they? Godwin is a sturdy man and Peg a well-fed woman. I have a fine dagger but Godwin surely has a blade also.

He'd not likely go upon the roads without one.

If I could force the family to return would they answer questions honestly, or continue their silence? And would a forced return be permanent or temporary? It would be difficult to lure an unhappy tenant into remaining in a place he did not want to be. And if Godwin thought his wife in peril he would be away again at his first opportunity.

I turned the palfrey and headed back to Bampton. 'Twas dark when I reached the castle, the drawbridge was raised and the portcullis down. The porter was not pleased when I shouted to him to reverse the tasks he had only a few moments earlier completed.

With the palfrey returned to the marshalsea I set off in the dark for Galen House. I would tell Lord Gilbert tomorrow that he had lost a tenant, and the rents the family provided. This would not be a happy duty, if Lord Gilbert's finances were as reduced as John Chamberlain suggested.

Wednesday dawned cold and gray, with low-hanging clouds and fog. Appropriate for the events which I would this day encounter.

I broke my fast with a stale maslin loaf and equally stale ale. This should have been a premonition. My first unpleasant task was to tell Lord Gilbert he had surely lost a tenant. He was not pleased. I had not supposed he would be.

"You followed Godwin nearly to Oxford?" he asked.

"Aye."

"Why not to the town, then?"

"Too many folk had traveled the road as I neared Oxford. I could no longer follow the cart wheels."

"Could you not have sought inns and found where the scoundrel planned to spend the night?"

"How many inns and hostels are found in Oxford?" I replied. "There must be thirty, mayhap more. 'Twould take a man two days to visit all of them."

"Oh. . . aye. . . likely."

"And if I found the family and could force them to return, how long would they remain?"

"Godwin will not find a better situation than he had here," Lord Gilbert growled.

"You remember I told you my opinion as to why the Tyrrells fled Bampton?"

"To protect the wife, you thought."

"Aye. And I may soon have enough evidence to charge her with murder."

"What complaint could she have had against Edmund Harkins?"

"I do not believe she acted upon her own grievance, nor did she act alone."

"With others? Who?"

"Beatrice Toty, Emmaline Parkin, and Leuca."

"What evidence have you for so serious an assertion?"

"Edmund Harkins was a brute."

"As all men know," Lord Gilbert interrupted. "You consider that evidence?"

"Not evidence – I'll review that in a moment – but cause. He had blackened Leuca's eye and split her eyebrow so badly I was required to stitch the cut only a few days before he disappeared.

"When Edmund was not seen for several days all assumed he had abandoned wife and family to begin a new life in some other place. Even Leuca thought this. So I believed at the time. But then pannaging pigs unearthed his corpse and foul murder was evident.

"I began to seek the man or men who slew Edmund, not considering at the time that women might be involved. A few days later a message was inscribed upon Galen House door with the point of a dagger. 'Leave it be.'

"A few days before Edmund blackened Leuca's eye I had walked the banks of Shill Brook seeking willow bark and monk's hood. Later I remembered that I had seen a place where monk's hood had been uprooted where I sought my own supply. Mayhap, I thought, the poison root of monk's hood was used to slay Edmund. I returned there to be sure of my memory.

"'Twas nearly dark when I returned to Galen House, but before I could gain my home three men, their faces obscured, emerged from a copse, seized me, and pitched me into the brook. One of these knaves said, 'Leave it be,' as was scratched into my door. The three were away before I could scramble from the stream. I had no chance to follow and discover who they were. But now I believe I know."

"Oh? Who?" Lord Gilbert asked.

"Stephen Parkin, Godwin Tyrrell, and Rolf Toty."

"These knew their wives had slain and buried Edmund Harkins?" Lord Gilbert asked.

"Aye. And but for ravenous pigs we would today believe Edmund in Abingdon or Banbury or mayhap even London, free of responsibility for wife and family. I believe there are others who know who slew Edmund but all are committed to silence."

"Who?"

"Father Harold, for one."

"But," Lord Gilbert said, "if he learned of the guilty through confession he would be pledged to silence. Was that the confession you believe he betrayed?"

"Mayhap. In his last sermon he spoke of an indemnity which would be required of sinful folk. Monday eve, after curfew, his clerk visited the Totys, Parkins, Tyrrells, and Leuca Harkins."

"To what purpose?"

"To collect the indemnity."

"You know this of a certainty?"

"Nay. Those Randall visited deny his call, and so also deny that coins changed hands."

"And now the priest is away with his loot," Lord Gilbert said, "so you cannot question him of the matter."

"He would not answer truthfully if I could. He threatened Stephen Parkin with disclosure of his wife's part in Edmund's slaying, demanding Parkin give up his daughter in return for silence.

"When I intervened, and you demanded he be removed from Bampton, he settled for coins in return for his silence."

"What of the man who pierced Uctred? Leuca's brother, was he not?"

"I suspect Leuca and the others did not approve of the man assaulting Uctred."

"Oh? Why not?"

"They might have slain me rather than fling me into Shill Brook. They did not. I believe they hoped to forestall my investigation without taking some extreme measure which would lead to greater inquiry. To stab one of your retainers would lead to more examination of Edmund's death, not less, and my death even more so. They hoped, I believe, that after a few weeks the murder would cease to be important to most folk, even me, and would be forgotten. After all, Edmund was a scoundrel and many of Bampton are pleased he is in the churchyard."

"You hesitated to arrest the man who attacked Uctred," Lord Gilbert said, "because you did not wish Leuca and others then unknown to know of your suspicions. Is this not so?"

"Aye."

"Will you now seize the fellow and charge him with wounding Uctred?"

"Aye. Who knows? Mayhap a threat of severe punishment will bring him to implicate those who slew Edmund. Then we will have proof where we now have but conjecture."

"'Tis admirable for a man to defend his sister," Lord Gilbert said. "I would do all in my power to protect Lady Joan."

"Then Ewen should have stabbed Edmund rather than Uctred. I will travel to Curbridge after my dinner and seize the man."

"Sir Reginald Stury is lord of Curbridge. The man is near bankrupt, I'm told. Gambles away his coin. Will wager snow on St. Swithin's Day if given odds. He'll not want to lose another tenant. Curbridge suffered much in the pestilence."

Kate and Adela had prepared this day a pottage of whelks, for 'twas a fast day. I would have no butter for my loaf. Adela seemed more cheerful than in past days. I assumed she knew that Father Harold was on his way to Exeter and would vex her no more. What else she might know which reduced her distress I could only guess.

Curbridge is but three miles from Bampton. I ate quickly as I was eager to set off for the village. 'Twas a mission I would have undertaken in the past with Arthur. Ewen was not a large or foreboding man, but even frail fellows will lash out at a man about to seize them. Especially if the result of the taking might be a walk to the scaffold.

Had I taken Arthur's son with me I might have saved time seeking Ewen's house. And he could have provided the muscle I would sorely need.

Lord Gilbert spoke true. Curbridge is much reduced. I counted five hearths and the decayed remains of six others. The manor house was little better than the dwellings of the tenants. Its thatching was rotted and chunks of daub had fallen from the walls. Sir Reginald is an impoverished knight with seemingly no opportunity to improve his fortune unless war with France resumes. Such poor knights see battle as a way to take prisoners which may be held for ransom. This is why peace is not viewed as a good thing, but rather as lamentable.

"What you want with Ewen?" Sir Reginald asked when he opened his door to my knock and learned whom I sought. Here was more evidence of his poverty. No servant answered my knock.

"I am Sir Hugh de Singleton, bailiff to Lord Gilbert at Bampton," I said.

"Heard of you. Why does Lord Gilbert's bailiff seek a tenant of mine?"

"The man attacked one of Lord Gilbert's grooms some days past and nearly slew him."

"You've come to seize him?"

"I have."

"Upon what evidence?"

"The man he pierced saw him limp as he fled from the attack. And the victim managed to draw his own dagger and slash it across Ewen's back as he fled. If you have seen your tenant recently you will have noticed that his cotehardie has been cut across the back and mended."

"Why would Ewen do such a felony?"

"To protect his sister."

"Leuca? Was Lord Gilbert's groom attempting to force himself upon her? Seems to me Ewen did a good thing, was this so."

"Nay. Nothing of the sort. Leuca's husband was a lout who often beat her. A few weeks past he was found slain. 'Tis my duty, repugnant as may be, to seek those who did the murder."

"Ewen?"

"Nay. Leuca and some friends, so I believe."

"Leuca slew her husband? The law pronounces that treason."

"Indeed. To protect her from the penalty Ewen sought to slay a man he thought might know of Leuca's guilt."

"And failed? The man has succeeded at little since a Frenchman chopped off part of his foot. 'Tis his excuse for incompetence."

"Which house is his?"

"Wait a moment. I'll take you there."

Sir Reginald disappeared into his manor house. I heard indistinct voices, then all became silent.

The knight did not soon reappear. When he did, two men came round the corner of the house at the same time. They held daggers before them, as did Sir Reginald. I was between three armed men who apparently resented my purpose.

As a lad I was quick. I had to be. I had three older brothers who delighted in pestering me. The only way to escape their unwanted attention was to outrun them. But Kate's cookery has thickened my waist and slowed my heels. And one of the men who appeared at the corner of the manor house was a wiry lad of perhaps eighteen years.

Three daggers pointed at a man will convince even the one who is witless that he is in danger. I took to my heels. The slender youth caught me about forty paces from the manor house. When he tackled me he lost his grip on his dagger, so I was not pierced. I rolled in the dirt, drew my own dagger, and rose to my knees to face Sir Reginald and the other lackey, who were close behind the lad who had tripped me up.

I was near to one of the decaying houses, so backed toward it, my dagger extended before me, so that I could be attacked from only one direction. Sir Reginald and his two grooms stopped several paces from me to consider what might be done next. I thought I knew why Sir Reginald had attacked me, and spoke of it.

"Curbridge is much reduced due to pestilence," I said. "Now you fear losing another tenant. Do you believe Lord Gilbert would allow you to slay me unavenged? He knows I have come here to arrest Ewen. If I do not return to Bampton in good time he will send some of his household knights to seek me."

"Bah," Sir Reginald scoffed. "I will tell his minions that you never arrived in Curbridge. Most likely rogues set upon you on the road. If they then seek Ewen he will be away, for I intend to tell him to be gone for a time. . . 'til Martinmas, mayhap, 'til this business blows over."

The road from Bampton curves round a copse of beech and oak trees a few hundred paces before entering Curbridge. Sir Reginald and his vassals had their backs to this road, but I could see clearly as two horsemen appeared around the bend. 'Twas Sir Jaket and Thomas.

Sir Reginald saw my eyes drawn to the road and turned to see what had caught my attention. His jaw dropped and his mouth fell open. He did not know Sir Jaket, I'm sure, but the sudden appearance of mounted men coming from the direction of Bampton could mean no good thing for his hastily contrived scheme.

"You are about to meet Sir Jaket Bec and Thomas, his squire," I said. "Sir Jaket is a household knight to Lord

Gilbert Talbot. He will be displeased at my reception in Curbridge. And I should mention that he is skilled in the use of a sword."

Sir Reginald and his henchmen lowered their daggers and backed away. About the time they did so Sir Jaket saw me, my back against the wall of a decaying house, facing three apparently hostile antagonists. He spurred his horse to a trot, Thomas close behind, and was in a trice close behind Sir Reginald.

"'Twas as Lord Gilbert feared," Sir Jaket said. "He knows Sir Reginald well and does not trust him. Told me to attend you in your mission else some mischief might follow. Said he should have advised you not to undertake seizing Ewen alone."

Sir Reginald and his vassals heard this while gingerly backing away. Their advantage in numbers was gone, and so was any desire for combat.

Sir Jaket had spoken loudly. Doors opened as residents not at work in the fields peered out to see what the tumult was about. One face I recognized. Ewen. The man saw my gaze fall upon him and vanished back into his house.

I would have liked to deal firmly with Sir Reginald, and with Lord Gilbert's authority behind me in the form of Sir Jaket's sword, I could have. But I had come to seize Leuca's brother and should not allow some personal slight to defeat my purpose.

I ran toward Ewen's house. Sir Jaket and Thomas, assuming a reason for haste and that I might need assistance, spurred their beasts and trotted after me. Sir Reginald and his minions were left to observe.

Ewen's house was of two bays, built when he or the previous inhabitant was more prosperous. So it was equipped with a rear door as well as a front. I threw open the front door in time to see Ewen fleeing out of the back. A woman – Ewen's wife, surely – stood open-mouthed in the first bay.

I ran toward the rear bay and the open door through which Ewen had disappeared. I heard Sir Jaket and Thomas close behind.

The rear bay of Ewen's house was evidently not constructed at the same time as the front. And the builder had included only one small skin window in the rear bay. So I did not see the difference in height of the floor of the second bay, caught a toe on the threshold, and fell headlong into the moldy straw. Sir Jaket and Thomas followed, and in less time than it takes to tell of the event we three were a tangle of arms and legs in the thresh. The woman laughed.

We sorted out knees and elbows belonging to each, regained our feet, and dashed for the rear door. From the opening I saw Ewen a hundred or more paces away, running across a field newly planted to rye. For a man with but half a foot at the end of a leg he was covering the ground with remarkable alacrity. The image of a scaffold in a man's imagination will work a marvelous increase to the speed of his feet.

Ewen was making for a wood which bordered the far side of the rye field. I set out after him, with Sir Jaket and Thomas close behind. The squire, being young and fleet and unencumbered by a sword, soon passed me and Sir Jaket. But as fast as he was it soon became clear that Ewen would gain the wood before Thomas could catch him. Thomas was yet fifty or so paces from Ewen when the fleeing fellow plunged into the forest and was lost to sight.

The collapse of Curbridge's population meant that if the village ever had a verderer it likely no longer did.

So no man cared for the forest. Fallen limbs would be gleaned for firewood, but even this would be affected by the reduced population. So 'twas easy for Ewen to lose himself in undergrowth and fallen branches. And lose himself he did.

I forged into the scrubby wood and saw no fleeing man even though trees and shrubs were nearly bare of foliage. I stopped, held out a hand to signal that Sir Jaket and Thomas should do likewise, and listened. If Ewen stumbled through undergrowth I thought I might track the sound of his passage. Not so. Either he stood silently against some tree or he had traveled so deeply into the wood the sound of his footsteps was lost.

"We must scatter," Sir Jaket said. "Thomas, you go to the dexter side; Sir Hugh, you go straight ahead, and I'll take the sinister way. Sing out if you see or hear the fellow."

I thought Sir Jaket's plan a good one. He and Thomas were soon lost to my sight as they searched their assigned routes, although I did occasionally hear what I thought was their footfall in the distance.

I stumbled through the forest for nearly a mile 'til I saw before me a lighter patch and came to the Witney road. To my right I saw Thomas, a hundred or so paces away. He had reached the road before me and had not cried out, so had not encountered Ewen. To my left the road was empty. But not for long. A moment later I saw Sir Jaket emerge from the forest, brushing clinging verdure and seeds from his cotehardie and chauces.

Knight and squire turned my way and approached. Across the road from the wood was an ancient stone wall, about waist high and overgrown with stonecrop and nettles. 'Twas low enough that a determined man could vault it and avoid clambering through the nettles.

I crossed the road and came near the wall. It enclosed a fallow field where sheep grazed, their droppings meant to fertilize the enclosure for next season's plowing and planting. The sheep cropped the grass placidly. No man had disturbed their browsing. A quick glance along the wall showed no man attempting to hide in the verdure.

The day was nearly done, my mission to Curbridge a failure. To return to the village and retrieve Sir Jaket's and Thomas's palfreys we must make our way through a darkening forest. I told my companions we must make haste, and we did. If Ewen was yet hidden in the wood he would have had no difficulty marking our passage.

In Curbridge I went to the manor house door and thumped vigorously upon it. There was no response. I shouted for Sir Reginald to appear. He did not. I shoved the unbarred door open and with Sir Jaket close behind, his sword unsheathed, I investigated the house. 'Twas vacant. The knight of Curbridge had fled.

I would tell Lord Gilbert of this troublesome encounter and allow my employer to decide what should be done with or to Sir Reginald. Gloom was settling over the realm. We would have to hurry to reach Bampton before dark.

Sir Jaket told me to mount his beast behind the saddle, so I was not required to walk home, but a horse's rump is not the most comfortable place from which to view the passing countryside.

I slid to the road at Church View Street, told Sir Jaket to inform Lord Gilbert that I would visit him in the morning, then made my way through the dark town to Galen House.

I called out to Kate and a moment later heard her raise the bar. She had not expected me to return so late, but had been wise enough to secure the house upon my eventual return.

My supper was a cold bowl of porre of peas. While I ate I told Kate of my failed attempt to apprehend Leuca's brother and the uncooperative knight of Curbridge.

"Would Leuca know where her brother might go to escape you?" Kate asked.

"If she did she'd not tell me."

"Ewen fled because he knew why you appeared at Curbridge?"

"No doubt."

"You think Leuca knows also?" Kate said.

"If she learns somehow that I traveled to Curbridge she will understand why."

"Then she played a part in Edmund's death."

"I am convinced of it."

"And others?"

"Peg Tyrrell, who with Godwin has absconded, Beatrice Toty, and Emmaline Parkin."

"Adela's mother did murder?"

"So I believe."

"And Adela knows it," Kate said. "Her behavior says so. How did four women overpower Edmund? Would he not cry out? Surely neighbors on Rosemary Lane would hear such a melee."

"Someone pulled monk's hood from a patch I know of just beyond the Weald. When I went there three or so weeks past to renew my supply of the root, I saw where some other had been there before me and drawn a few plants from the soil."

"If Edmund was poisoned 'twould not require four women to overcome him," Kate said.

"Aye. But to transport his corpse to a hidden place in a wood might. And he was not taken far. Far enough that 'twas thought he would not be found, no farther."

"And but for the swine he'd be there yet," Kate shuddered. "Think you other folk of Bampton know this?"

"Aye. 'Tis why you and I have received the cold shoulder of late. How many know? I've no idea. But I'd reckon more than a few."

"What will happen if you charge Leuca, Emmaline, and Beatrice with slaying Edmund? Would the King's Eyre convict them?"

"Mayhap. But likely not. 'Tis mostly conjecture. One thing is certain. If I send them before a judge the town will turn against me and we will lose our place here. Lord Gilbert would see no other path but to replace me."

"Would you ignore injustice for our welfare?"

"Nay. But many would argue Edmund's death to be no injustice."

"And you?" Kate asked.

"I am of two minds. Should four women have slain the brute who mistreated one of them? Nay. Should they go to a scaffold for their deed? Nay, also."

I went to my Bible chest, lifted the book and found the words of the prophet Micah. Kate watched patiently. My wife has no Latin, so when I found the verse I sought, I read a translation to her: "'What doth the LORD require of thee but to do justly, and to love mercy, and to walk humbly with thy God?' The prophet enjoins us to do justice and love mercy. But in the matter of Edmund Harkins' death how am I to do both? Justice requires his slayers be accountable for making of him a corpse. Mercy demands they be pardoned."

Kate was silent, considering my predicament. Our predicament, for her future as well as my own would hinge upon my decision.

"Mayhap," she finally said, "Lord Gilbert will have an opinion."

"He will, assuredly. Great men always have opinions."

"Which it is safest to heed," Kate added.

"Indeed. I will explain tomorrow to Lord Gilbert how matters stand. He may not directly charge me with the course I must follow, but I have become skilled at reading his mood."

"And what do you think that will be?"

"He will hate the loss of a tenant if Leuca, Emmaline, and Beatrice hang. Emmaline and Beatrice's husbands will remain the bishop's tenants, so Lord Gilbert will not lose more than he already has, but for Leuca."

"But Emmaline's and Beatrice's husbands will not be so profitable to the bishop if they work alone," Kate said. "Marriage is an enterprise in which two become one, but in truth three – in their efficiency and value to the lord of their manor."

I slept fitfully that night, as, I believe, did Kate. Her turning and tossing did not awaken me. For most of the night I was already wakeful. When I did sleep it was to dream of women standing upon a scaffold, a jeering throng heaping abuse upon them.

Adela appeared shortly after dawn. The threat Father Harold had posed was gone, yet she seemed heavy of heart. I was sure I knew why. As she busied herself about the kitchen I saw her observe me from the corner of her eye, intent upon my demeanor without appearing so to be.

I shared a tasteless maslin loaf with Kate, then set off for the castle and a meeting I would have preferred to avoid. I found Lord Gilbert, Richard, Charles, Sir Jaket,

Thomas, and two other of Lord Gilbert's household knights preparing for a hunt. If they were successful a haunch of venison would soon be hanging in the castle larder.

My employer would not be pleased to put off his hunt to hear what I had to say. Nor would he be happy with my words. I felt doubly cursed. Meanwhile, as I crossed the castle yard the fewterer brought four lymers from their kennels. The dogs knew what was about to happen and began to bark and whimper excitedly.

Lord Gilbert's back was to me as I entered the castle yard. He mounted his beast, pulled upon the reins to turn the animal, then saw me striding across the castle yard. He frowned, guessing that my appearance could mean no good thing. He slid from the saddle, handed the reins to a groom, and awaited my approach. The others of the hunting party looked from me to Lord Gilbert to each other and shrugged. Even the dogs seemed to lose their ardor.

"Have you tidings for me of Edmund Harkins' slayers, or are you yet baffled? Sir Jaket said you have news for me of your visit to Curbridge."

I looked to the stairs to the solar, tilted my head, and he divined my meaning.

"Return the hounds to the kennels and the horses to the stables," he said. "We will wait 'til after dinner to go ahunting."

While others hastened to obey his commands, I followed Lord Gilbert up the stairs to the solar. He closed the door behind us, took his upholstered chair, motioned to another chair for me, then called for John Chamberlain.

John must have been close by. In an instant he appeared in the door leading to the hall stairs.

"Send a groom with wood for the fire," Lord Gilbert commanded. "The hunt is postponed 'til after dinner."

John bowed, backed from the room, and I heard his footsteps quick upon the stone as he descended the stairs in search of a groom.

"When we spoke two days past," Lord Gilbert began, "you thought you knew who had slain Edmund Harkins. Do you?"

"Aye."

"Then seize them and I'll send them to the Sheriff of Oxford to await the King's Eyre."

"I am sure of my suspicions, but mayhap the evidence will not be convincing to a judge."

"Why so?"

"I have no witnesses to the murder except for those who did the felony, and if they remain silent, as they will, all else is conjecture."

"'Tis the three women you suspect, then?"

"Four, including Peg Tyrrell, whose husband has taken her from Bampton."

"You believe the others may also flee?"

"They may."

"And even should they not, if the king's judges find them guilty I am out of a tenant."

"And the bishop will lose two."

"Bah. 'Tis not his purse I am concerned for. So what is to be done? What do you recommend?"

"Nothing."

"Nothing? You suggest a perversion of justice?"

"There is a passage in the book of the prophet Micah which reads, 'What doth the LORD require of thee, but to do justly, and to love mercy, and to walk humbly with thy God?' Here is the rub. Can justice and mercy both be done?"

"What say you, Hugh?"

"I prefer others face justice, but seek mercy for myself."

"And for the women who slew Edmund Harkins? This is why you suggest nothing be done to them? You will seem incompetent, you know, if Bampton folk believe you could not identify murderers when rumors of the guilty will be bandied about."

"Mayhap. But a sullied reputation can be reclaimed. A neck stretched at the end of a hempen rope cannot be. And as for rumors of who slew Edmund, these are already current. I'm sure of it."

"Villagers will protect their own, eh?"

"Aye. Though was the shoe on the other foot and Edmund had slain Leuca he would not have found folk turning a blind eye to the felony."

The groom appeared with logs for the fire and with a poker proceeded to prod the embers to life. Our conversation died as the groom worked. Lord Gilbert stroked his beard, considering what was known and what was supposition.

When the fire was blazing vigorously the groom bowed, backed from the room, and closed the door. Lord Gilbert remained silent, staring into the fire. I awaited his decision.

"What of Leuca's brother?" he said. "What was his name?"

"Ewen."

"He tried to slay Uctred. Is he also to go unpunished?"

"Did Sir Jaket tell you yesterday that we were unable to take Ewen? He saw us, guessed the reason for our appearance in Curbridge, and disappeared into a wood. Darkness ended our search for the man."

"Sir Jaket said that Sir Reginald was unhelpful. Did he aid Ewen's escape? I'll deal with him. With enough pressure he'll find Ewen and send him to me."

"'Twould be best if he did not," I said.

"Why so?"

"If Leuca's brother hangs for attempting to end Uctred's life, her own guilt in her husband's death will become clear to even a buffoon. And once more, I may be seen as knowing of her felony and doing nothing about it. If Ewen is not apprehended I can maintain a pretext of ignorance in Edmund's death."

Lord Gilbert went to stroking his beard again. "I like nothing of this business," he finally said.

"Nor do I. We have been presented with several bad choices and 'tis up to us to choose the least objectionable. Life is not always about choosing the good over the bad, or even the best over the good."

"Hah," Lord Gilbert continued the thought. "Or the bad over the worst."

Unsolved felonies oft reappear and bite the miscreants responsible. But if such a happenstance occurs in the matter of Edmund Harkins 'twill be some time in the future. "Sufficient to the day is the evil thereof." I will worry about revealed felons some other day.

My reputation did indeed suffer for a time. But evil is never absent for long, and when felony next appeared in Bampton I recovered my fame as a sleuth. And as a surgeon, for I not only discovered who had cracked a priest's skull when he objected to a theft, but reassembled the pieces and saved his life.

Afterword

Many readers of the chronicles of Hugh de Singleton have asked about medieval remains in the Bampton area. St. Mary's Church is little changed from the fourteenth century. The May Bank Holiday is a good time to visit Bampton. The village is a Morris dancing center, and on that day hosts a day-long Morris dancing festival.

Village scenes in the popular television series *Downton Abbey* were filmed on Church View in Bampton. The town library became the Downton hospital, and St. Mary's Church appeared in several episodes.

Bampton Castle was, in the fourteenth century, one of the largest castles in England in terms of the area enclosed within the curtain wall. Little remains of the castle but for the gatehouse and a small part of the curtain wall, which form a part of Ham Court, a farmhouse in private hands. The current owners are doing extensive restoration work, including restoring a part of the moat.

Gilbert Talbot was indeed the lord of the manor of Bampton in the late fourteenth century.

Mel Starr

WHAT'S YOUR NEXT HUGH DE SINGLETON NOVEL?

Prince Edward's Warrant

The chronicles of Hugh de Singleton, surgeon

MEL STARR

Author of *The Unquiet Bones*

ISBN: 978 1 78264 262 6

e-ISBN: 978 1 78264 263 3

Without a Trace

The chronicles
of Hugh de Singleton,
surgeon

MEL STARR

Author of *The Unquiet Bones*

ISBN: 978 1 78264 267 1
e-ISBN: 978 1 78264 268 8

ISBN: 978 1 78264 306 7

e-ISBN: 978 1 78264 307 4

Master Wycliffe's Summons

The chronicles of Hugh de Singleton, surgeon

St J

MEL STARR

Author of *The Unquiet Bones*

ISBN: 978 1 78264 347 0

e-ISBN: 978 1 78264 348 7